SWORDMEN OF VISTAR

by

CHARLES NUETZEL

The Borgo Press
An Imprint of Wildside Press

MMVII

CONTENTS

To

A damsel named

Heidi Garrett

Who is a dear friend

FOREWORD

I would like to warn the reader that there are few of you who will believe the following story of Thoris of Haldolen and his encounter with the Wizard of Zorkada. It is of little importance, since I am presenting the manuscript to the publisher as fiction. There is no way to provide solid proof that the original manuscript is authentic nor that Thoris of Haldolen was a real man who lived some 15 to 30,000 years ago as the Warrior General of God-Lord Muda of Haldolen.

I cannot myself honestly claim that I find it easy to accept the story of Thoris of Haldolen as fact; any more than I can claim to accept unconditionally that there was a continent in the Pacific Ocean which some modern men have falsely labeled Mu—for lack of the true name. Only one thing can I claim: to accept the authority of the man who sent the manuscript to me.

But let me relate the circumstances surrounding my possession of the translation of this manuscript and my acquaintance with a man I shall call Professor John Davis Bradford. He was a well-known doctor of archeology, searcher into the ancient ruins of lost civilizations, chaser of obscure facts and rumors. I have checked into the man's past and found it flawless of any sort of scandal or suggestion of fraud. The verity of the manuscript must in the long run rest on Professor Bradford's shoulders. I believe that he was convinced of its authenticity.

Some years ago I met Prof. John Bradford when he was giving a lecture on ancient ruins, mainly concerning the lost continent of Mu. His talk was an expose of the Mu which James Churchward had originally "researched" and "proven" many years before. Mu was, according to Churchward, a lost continent which sank in the Pacific Ocean; being the Birthplace of Mankind and the original Garden of Eden. Many science fiction authors have used his books as the springboard for fictional novels about "Mu".

After the lecture I was given the opportunity to have a private conversation with Prof. Bradford, having been introduced to him by a mutual friend, Dr. Walter Daugherty. After that we communicated at some length for several years. Then I lost track of Prof. Bradford in the mid-50s. Late in 1960 I received a letter from him dated from the South Pacific, a portion of which follows:

"I should imagine you have wondered about me during the past years. But you will wonder far more when I tell you I have found remarkable evidence of a lost civilization in the Pacific Ocean. I will not call it the Mu of Churchward fame, for there is no evidence to connect that man's research with what I have discovered. That Churchward believed there was a continent in the Pacific Ocean could only be one of those strange elements of chance, a freak accident; or...maybe a fantasy or dream which he wished were real and was able to sell to an uncritical public. Nevertheless I believe this manuscript tells not of Churchward's Mu but of another—far more real—world which actually existed long before our modern civilization came into being.

"I had been digging in one of the smaller, lesser known islands and found a—well, what could one call it other than a time-capsule: it is a three foot-square block of strange hardened material—which is neither metal nor stone—surrounded by an unknown substance that is a variety of metal I have not seen before (upon which is etched fine, delicate carvings of oddly dressed men and women). In this I found a manuscript written on an extremely fine, coated paper-like material. Nothing more was in the compartment. Possibly some advanced science—or another branch unknown to our civilization—made it possible for the manuscript to survive the 15-30,000 years it must have lain there waiting to be discovered. But that is of little matter. I found it; it survived.

"With computers at the University I have isolated the writing as being a very ancient one. My guess is that it is the root of all our ancient languages. If so, it might give some hint to a few we have not been able to translate. The amazing thing is that the translation is quite simple once you get on with it.

"I am sending you the first part of this script—my translation—and a couple of photos. Since you have shown much curiosity in such things, and because you are something of a writer, I thought maybe you could polish my style and fix up the little matters of narrative which a total amateur like myself have found impossible to handle."

The rest of the letter had little to do with the immediate subject, other than to add that the professor planned on returning to the island of the time-capsule to do some more digging and then investigate some clues which he had discovered in the original manuscript but left unrevealed in the part which he sent me.

In a matter of weeks I received a rather bulky package. In it was a rough hand-written manuscript and a couple of Photostats as promised. One of these pictures reveals a detailed map with strange writings on it, which the professor translated on the margins. The other was merely a picture of the first page of the original manuscript, beautifully "printed"—I can only guess that this was either some form of typewriting or printing; but we will probably never know.

I read the manuscript with great excitement and interest, though in the end it was almost impossible to believe even this evidence. Yet knowing the professor as I have and realizing his professional reputation, I found it difficult to believe this to be a hoax.

I have several professional scientific opinions about the Photostat of the first page of manuscript which do little to support the fact that this is even a translatable text. But the professor was noted for knowing more about ancient languages than any other living person in the world. Yet was he merely another Churchward, making reality out of fantasy? Probably I will never know for sure, for he has once more disappeared.

The Professor had placed a short note with the manuscript to the effect that he would contact me shortly. Since I have not heard from him in the last few years it must be assumed that he has met with some kind of death.*

Still each reader must decide for himself whether to believe the text of this story for Thoris of Haldolen.

But a few words of explanation as to the style of the story itself and what I have done with the original material might be of interest before closing. It was a very lengthy and involved story with many details which have been cut down. I have, where possible, attempted to modernize the Professor's original translation and fill in some minor gaps which he left questionable. But beyond that, the following is a faithful presentation of the manuscript which Prof. Bradford sent me.

I can only hope that the reader will find a few diverting hours of pleasure following the adventures of Thoris of Haldolen.

—Charles Nuetzel
Thousand Oaks, California
July 2006

An update concerning these matters is in the newly added Epilogue.

APOLOGIA

I am Thoris of Haldolen, Warrior General of the God-Lord of Haldolen, Muda XI, our God and Ruler. I was born of the common stock of food growers. When I entered the Academy of Death there was no indication that I might rise to the position of Warrior General. I was in the beginning a student in the Commoner Corps, entering at the age of 40 seasons. This was a position not conducive to progress to the Rank of Officer. Seldom is a Commoner given the chance to go beyond that of Officer Ten or work his way up to Officer One; once a member of the Commoner Corps, always thus until death ends all that was or is in the blackness of eternity.

I will not bore those who know of my life with such details recorded elsewhere but will lay down the total of my early adventures with the Ijans, in the lands of Jorjos, which led to me returning Illa, the daughter of our God-Lord, to her father.

CHAPTER ONE

AT THE SEA GOD'S MERCY

The galley ship *Vayis* was three days out to sea on its way around the continent of Haldolen, when the tragic storm struck unexpectedly. I was posted in front of the door which led to the chambers of Princess Illa, daughter of God-Lord Muda, as was my assigned duty. The morning had run its normal course; Rusis, Warrior Class One in charge of the warriors who manned the galley *Vayis*, had awakened me at the first breath of morning when Fahda the Sun ended darkness. A quick bowl of warm mush served as my morning meal, then I went up on deck, across the ship, passed the hundred oarsmen and stepped to the far side of the *Vayis*, where Princess Illa and her chambermaids were quartered in the back of the galley. There I took my post as personal guard to the Princess.

The ocean air had that salty smell which is so refreshing early in the morning. There was no sign or hint of what would take place in only a short time and be the beginning of a harrowing adventure in the lands of Jorjos. The sky was clear and colorful in the morning sunlight.

This was my third day at sea and I still thrilled to the coolness, the odor and the endless water stretching out in all directions, lighted in bright orange-reds by Fahda the Sun coming up from the East. The ocean was all new to me, since I had spent all my eighty-two seasons in Rota, where I had been born.

Just five days before I had been in my beloved Rota, just twelve seasons out of the Rota Academy of Death where

11

I had learned to become a well-trained warrior. During these twelve Seasons I had moved from Warrior Class Ten to Warrior Class Six, which allowed me six men-at-arms as my personal unit. I had done battle under the warrior unit color of white against members of the Rota Red and Rota Green units, always victorious. This had served to move me up the ranks much faster than my fellow warriors. So when the Warrior General was searching for candidates to man and guard the ship *Vayis* on which Princess Illa was to be taken to visit her cousin Sahdie on the Eastern shores of Haldolen, he heard my name and picked me as one of Illa's personal guard.

The appointment was a great honor, and my excitement even greater as I had started out for the city of Muda, after receiving blessings from the Goddess Rota, upon whom I had also brought honor. I had lived in her lands all my life and this was to be my first trip away from the place of my birth.

I traveled by public coach-rail. It took half a day to go the distance between the temple-city to Rota to that of the Capitol of Haldolen, Muda. The rolling hills of our beautiful continent were fascinating at first, but then grew tiresome. Lands of the food-growers stretched out almost as far as one could see in each direction, painting the hills with rows of green and yellow.

My excitement at going to the city of Muda built to bursting when I saw the peak of the Temple of Muda, a huge golden structure measured to be the height of twenty men. This huge monument to our First God-Lord Muda is such that it brings a true sense of wonder to all who look upon it. First the tip of the pyramid showed over the rolling hills which surrounded Muda, then slowly the golden peak rode higher and higher as we climbed over the last hill before overlooking the Capitol of Haldolen.

The sight which met my eyes upon seeing our beloved city of Muda was breathtaking. Where Rota is only a gathering of Temple, marketplace, Academy of Death, the Warriors' living quarters and general government buildings, the city of Muda seemed an endless expanse of buildings stretching outward as far as I could see. The city reached from the ocean upon which the docks rested, holding to their huge sail boats, war and passenger galleys; then surged inland across the lands toward the walled palace and Temple of God-Lord Muda. Behind the walls of the Temple I could see the glorious statue of First God-Muda, the arched form of his body, arms stretched up high into the sky in holy worship to the Sun, God-Fahda, that glistening golden ball of heat and life which travels across the skies at day and sleeps beyond the edge of the world at night.

For only a moment the coach-rail hesitated, giving me this one magnificent view of the city below, with its high towers, its patchwork of buildings, cut by long straight streets running like the rays of Fahda from the Temple of Muda to the surrounding city in all directions. Then the coach moved down the hill and the view became more restricted as we entered the city itself.

I was garbed in the standard warrior one-piece undergarment which went down just above the knees—colored white—over which was my leather harness that supported short sword, knife sheaths and hook for the long sword sheath on my left side. The leather was plain brown, as it should be for a commoner; one strap went over my right shoulder, with one silver oval upon which was deeply impressed the number six, placed over my heart.

The buildings of Muda were made of brick, painted over in various bright colors. Windows, some six heads from the ground, were gaily sprinkled with flower displays. There was a buzz of activity which I had never heard in Rota. This was the heart of our civilization, an Empire which was stretching her borders outward across the world, conquering savage uncivilized lands which existed beyond the waters of the Haldolen Ocean. Our colonies had for hundreds of summers thrived upon the foreign lands discovered by our great explorers. And Muda was Capital of all the Haldolen Empire—greatest of all Empires the world over.

The coach-rail passed a huge, crowded market place, where countless stalls were laden with food, jewelry, amulets, pottery, metal works, tools, weapons, livestock, baskets, snake charms, furniture, and all things which might be offered for sale to the average family. It was a loud, smelly

13

place where the stink of human sweat mingled with that of fish and animals—both live and newly killed. The shouting of voices, the calling of chants as merchants attempted to market their wares, became a mass sound swelling loud and then fading as we moved beyond the plaza area where the market was set up. Then we came to what is known as Bots Area because of the many establishments which serve Bots or other forms of liquor and offer the services of half-naked young girls.

I gathered the small bag which contained such private and valuable possessions as I might need on such a long trip: The Stone of Rota, to protect me against the evils of death; the Cross of Rota, to bring me back home in safety. I then stood and worked my way out of the coach.

I had been instructed that somebody would meet me. Now, for the first time since leaving Rota, I felt terribly alone, defenseless and most of all very unimportant and small in a big city.

Suddenly a man, dressed in Red, wearing the oval of Warrior One on his harness strap, stepped up to me, smiled. He gripped my arm in the standard greeting of Haldolen, and introduced himself as Rusis, in charge of the warriors of the *Vayis*.

He was dark-haired, square-jawed, brown-eyed—quite my opposite; I am blond and blue-eyed. He was half a head shorter than myself but more stocky. For a large man, he looked quite graceful and able to handle himself in a battle. I was to learn that he was a fine fighting man. He had been in the service of Muda for ten four-seasons and expected to move to Officer Ten, which was quite impressive.

Rusis took me to a large galley tied to the docks in the harbor of Muda. The galley was decorated with gold trimmings and spotted with countless jewels of many brilliant colors. This was the *Vayis*, a 100-oar vessel, flying the personal flag of Muda, upon which was the golden pyramid of our beloved God-Lord. Such was my introduction to the galley which would take me almost to the shores of Jorjos. High were the *Vayis'* sails, the huge double mast reaching some eight men upwards into the sky, its huge crimson sail now strapped tight into place around the crossbeams.

14

The *Vayis* was typical of all large galleys, except that the First Officer's quarters was in this case turned into a compartment for Illa and her chambermaids. For this was the private galley of the daughter of Muda. Below her compartment was the supply hole. The sleeping quarters for warriors and officers was located at the opposite end of the galley. The slaves, as usual, slept at their oars below and between the front and back of the ship.

I was given a quick tour of the *Vayis* and allowed to look into the chambers of Princess Illa's cabin. It was flowing with filmy cloth draped from the middle of its ceiling and coming to rest at the four walls. A golden table sat in the middle of the room, carved with beautiful designs of flowers and vines, and a low, large bed centered on the far wall.

"You will be posted in front of the door during the first half day and the first half night. You will be relieved by warrior Gart," Rusis informed me as he closed the door.

And thus it was that I happened to be in the front of Princess Illa's sleeping chambers when the black storm struck the third day out at sea, far from the shores of Haldolen, with the coast of Jorjos just over the eastern horizon.

This morning, like the two before, all my thoughts were centered on the mental image of Illa, beautiful daughter of our Ruler. This image had plagued me from the first moment I laid eyes upon her, when she arrived on board at midday, just before sailing from the harbor of Muda.

Illa had been dressed in a drapery of fine linen of blue which fell gently around her full graceful body, adding an air of royal magnificence to her already breathtaking appearance. Her blond hair floated over rounded shoulders and slender arms. Full lips held a slight, formal smile as she nodded to the line of warriors of which I was a member. From that moment on I was in love with Illa.

So this third morning out to sea, like those before, my thoughts were dreams of Illa.

At first the weather was calm and clear, then slowly the ocean began to balloon up around the *Vayis*. The wind pressed hard against the sails, the galley seemed to creak, strain in anguish. The day abruptly turned ugly with great black clouds smothering Fahda the Sun and gathering a

15

darkness together as if night had descended unexpectedly on the world. The ocean swelled high and rose above the sides of the *Vayis* like hungry arms attempting to drown all those on board. The greedy waters swept over the galley slaves, then slowly drained away as if reluctant to leave the screaming, terrified men. The winds grew in hateful force, violently tore at the straining sails, ripping, shredding the thick canvas as if it were made of thin paper. The screeching moans of the *Vayis*, as the boards fought against one another, cracked loud in the air as the galley fought to save its passengers from the swirling watery depths below. The screams of oarsmen, chained to their places, knifed in my ears as I stood there, grasping the handrail in front of me, dazed by the sudden, unexpected storm which had fallen upon the world without any warning, as if an evil spell of some great Wizard had been brought into being.

A loud, horrifying snap sounded from above. The *Vayis* screamed in agony as its upper arms were torn in two. The huge splintered mast shuddered downward and then swung viscously to the right, to fall directly toward the cabin in which Princess Illa was secured.

My nerves cried out silently, every thought, every muscle strained to discover some way to save the daughter of Muda. But there was no time to act. I was paralyzed.

Time split, frozen, and then surprisingly the breath of the wind-gods grasped the falling mast and flung it sideways. It slammed into the edge of the cabin, shuddered, tilted, and shot into the ocean like an arrow slicing through the air.

Screams sounded from inside the Princess' cabin. The door abruptly swung open and Illa stood there, face drained white, lips compressed, but a stubborn, brave expression burning in her green eyes.

Her lips opened, as if to say something, then before either of us could move, two things happened at once. The galley tilted madly downwards and on its side; the Princess was pushed out past the door. Then a huge wave covered the *Vayis*, smashing over me and the Princess. My only thought was to find Illa, save her. But I could not even protect myself against the twisting current of the powerful waters.

I felt a form smash against me, then arms, legs, tangled round my body. It was impossible to do more than grasp what I knew to be Illa. It was like some nightmare hell, and neither of us had a chance to even realize what was actually taking place. I believed the water would pass over us, that in a moment we would be sprawled on the deck, wet, panting, but safe.

I grabbed for Illa and for the rail at the same time, and then suddenly the world spun. My lungs clamped tight, bursting for air; my mouth filled with salt water as we twisted upside down, each clinging to one another as the world turned into an angry oceanic pit of blackness and sucked us down into its depths like a monstrous hungry mouth attempting to devour us alive.

I had heard stories about death by drowning, being told that it is the most pleasant way to eternity, like dying in the arms of a sea goddess. But from what I experienced in those first moments, completely buried under the churning mass of the ocean, it was hard to believe such claims. My lungs seemed to catch fire, convulse. My body felt as if it were about to burst under the rushing pressure. Death squeezed at me with awful hands, clawed fingers clamped hard about my throat, mouth, lungs.

Yet all this time I struggled to keep hold of Illa, while fighting to reach the surface. The instinct of survival is so great that even in a moment when death attacks, one battles for a single second more of life with no thought beyond that immediate need.

The chilled waters encased my body hard on all sides. My muscles strained in a mad attempt to bring the two of us to the surface, if but for a moment, so that air might relieve the pressure crushing our lungs.

I felt Illa squirm, writhe against me, her arms clasped around my neck; and I was, even in those desperate moments, aware of the pressure of her soft, feminine form. But that shudder made it clear that possibly it was already too late.

Then I felt my head clear the water and at the same time I jerked the Princess upward into the air.

My lungs gasped automatically, yet all attention was centered on the woman. Was she still alive or had it been too late?

But I did not immediately receive my answer because we were plunged under a huge wave. This time, though, I was prepared, and went with the current, calmly working my way upward. In moments we broke the surface once more.

I heard Illa gasp and a hot thrill waved through me as a realization came that she was alive.

Immediately I began a mental search for some plan of action; some way to survive the storm and return to the *Vayis*.

Before it was possible to take even more than two healthy gulps of air, we were once more sucked under a wave. This time the current and force were considerably weaker. When we surfaced, the ocean was less turbulent, the wind tired, the sky already beginning to open to the hot rays of Fahda the Sun. But there was yet a long struggle before us, for the storm had not totally given up on claiming our bodies for its watery grave.

For some time we pitted our frail bodies against the powerful sea, again and again being pulled under, only to fight once more to surface. But each time the sky seemed brighter, the black evil clouds split wider apart, until finally we were able for the most part to keep floating, rising and falling with the less violent waves.

The first thing I did was search for the *Vayis*. Then I saw it far away, out beyond calling distance. It tossed and rolled with the abating storm, drifting farther and farther from us. By the time its crew even realized the loss of their Princess it would be too late. Even then the galley might not be in any condition to return and make a search. Our fate was totally in the hands of the ocean-gods.

I knew that we would soon die if there wasn't a way to keep ourselves afloat long enough to reach land—a likelihood which I could not believe to be even vaguely feasible. But we had to keep trying, regardless of how hopeless it might seem.

I turned my attention to the woman. I was still clutching her close so there would be no chance of becoming separated. "Are you all right...Princess Illa?"

For a few moments she didn't answer. Then her voice whispered weakly: "Yes. Now what?"

She nodded toward the *Vayis*, indicating that she also realized how futile were our chances.

"We will...find a way. The gods willing." I felt that these were hollow and meaningless words. How could we possibly survive for more than a short time? Land was beyond the horizon, a distance which not even the best swimmer could make. And even that land was Jorjos, where the people of Ijans lived—enemies of Haldolen. We knew little of the land of Jorjos, only that its borders had always been hostile to our explorers.

Still, any land would have been welcomed.

It was then that I saw something in the ocean some distance from us. My first reaction was that it must be a sea monster which would happily devour us as a mid-morning snack.

Instinctively my right hand flexed, as if to reach for a sword that should have been strapped to my left side but which had fallen into the ocean, sheath and all. Then I automatically realized the uselessness of fighting, for any sword would seem but a pick against some monstrous creature.

As I prepared myself to give up all hope, my eyes took in more details of the strange object. I expected it to raise upwards, turn in snarling attack. But it merely floated lazily on the crest of a wave. Then all of a sudden we were dropped into a valley between two mountain waves, and our heads submerged under water.

As I gasped air a moment later, my mind still pictured the object which had floated on the ocean. Then the water rose and I saw it once more. This time it pointed towards the skyline like some headless monster's neck, and for the first time I realized what it was: the splintered mast of the *Vayis*—that which was directly responsible for Illa having been swept overboard with me!

What an ironic humor the Gods must have.

A shout of joy burst from my lips and I swallowed salt water as we were once more covered. When surfaced, Illa shook the water from her face and frowned up at me, her lips just under mine.

"What happened? Why'd you shout?" Her voice was tight with fear, high-pitched.

"The mast—out there! If we can swim to it—it...will be something...to hold on to. A...chance to reach...land!" I had turned her around and pointed, while speaking, all the time struggling to keep both our heads above water.

She sucked in air. "Do you...really think..."

"Here...on my back! Put...your arms around my...neck. We'll swim!" I offered, between mouthfuls of salt water.

Illa hesitated, started to object, then did as told. I could imagine how hard she found it to follow orders from a mere common warrior. But this was not the time to argue and it was a credit to her that she realized the fact and acted upon it.

The mast was at least the length of fifteen men from us when I first spotted in. By now the distance seemed twice as far. I am not a bad swimmer, and in fact ranked among the top ten of my fellow warriors in Rota; but my body was now tired from the struggle against the water. That, mixed with the weight of Illa—even though she is quite light—and with the waters which were still attempting to engulf us, made the distance seem insurmountable. As it was, the mast itself was moving away from us.

Many times I had to rest. Many more times we were swallowed by the ocean, only to fight up to the surface. But time was in one way on our side, since the storm was already passing, drifting to the South towards the frozen lands beyond the Haldolen Ocean.

How long it took to get to where the mast had been when first spotted I could not even guess. But Fahda the Sun had moved in the sky by the time I came within a body length of my destination. By then I was too exhausted to think. My mind was paralyzed, reduced to the single goal: the mast! I felt no joy, no release, no emotional response at all. My arms cut forward again and again, moving through

20

the water, reaching towards the taunting wooden shaft which seemed to pull away in a perverse effort to keep just beyond reach.

Then a gasp sounded from Illa and my fingers touched wood. I was hardly aware of contacting anything. The weight of Illa's body released from my neck and back; but I didn't have the strength to find out why. The next awareness was that of lying across the mast, arms touching water on one side, legs plunged in deep on the other. If a moment passed, or if a long time lapsed, I don't know.

Abruptly I remembered that Princess Illa had slipped from my back and into the water.

My eyes blinked open. I cried out weakly, calling her name.

"I'm here, Warrior," came a lilting voice in answer to my call.

I struggled to get myself in a position to see Illa. Once in the water up to my chest, holding on to the mast, I saw her. She was on the opposite side. Her face smiled expectantly as she looked at me. She was only an arm's distance away, hair matted tightly around her slender, lovely face.

"We made it!" she cried jubilantly, like a little child who has been given hope when there is no reason for hope and believes that this alone solves all their problems.

But hope was not enough. I knew that much. We would need food, water. And even with food and water there was no real chance of survival. The ocean itself would grow icy during the night. We would die of exposure, of freezing. Hunger and thirst were the least of our worries. Then there was always the possibility of sea monsters, known to down whole galleys in one gulp of their mighty, fang-lined jaws.

What hope was there! What prospect did we have of even surviving one night, let alone reaching the shores of Jorjos? And even if we were to make it to Jorjos, what chance did we have of returning to our beloved land of Haldolen? We would have to travel many days' march to reach the Haldolen colonies to the south.

Still I did not have it in my heart to press the point home to Princess Illa. She was now living in pure hope, and that alone would make her last moments at least more bearable. If things got too painful, too hopeless, it would always be possible to end her torture with a knife. But until then, maybe I would have a short time to be with the woman I loved. Maybe that was worth dying for—I was sure it would be.

"Yes, we made it," I managed, holding back the heavy sense of irony from my voice, "we made it."

CHAPTER TWO

IN NAYPEAN'S DOMAIN

The ocean spread out around us in all directions, seemingly endless; light-blue glass which flickered in the sunlight like bright diamonds. The sun had drifted down toward the East. The water was almost calm now—the storm had passed.

In order to have something to do, more than anything else, I began to work my way along the mast, carefully examining it. What I expected to find I don't know. Illa asked what I was doing. I merely grunted unintelligibly and continued.

The mast was made of rough wood and had been badly splintered toward the base. As I worked my way up to the tip of the shaft, I saw a snake-like object floating lazily in the water, and the shredded remains of a small portion of the *Vayis*' sail. Immediately I shouted in surprise at this discovery.

"What did you find?" Princess Illa called.

"Rope!" Instinctively I knew this was what I had been looking for.

"Oh? What good is that out here in the middle of the ocean?" Illa sounded disappointed, annoyed.

"We can tie ourselves to the mast. It will at least prevent the possibility of falling asleep and slipping into the ocean. Or getting separated from the mast." I grabbed the rope, slipped the short sword from my sheath, which had amazingly stayed in place—the knife and long sword having found a grave in the depths below sometime during our struggles to keep alive.

23

Taking the thick rope, I moved along the mast to where the Princess was.

"Here." I handed her one end of the rope. "Take this and tie it around your waist—loosely into a Muda-knot, so that it will be easy enough to slip out of in an emergency, but not so loose that it will work its way off without your help."

As I spoke, I pulled the other end of the rope around the mast, made a slip-knot and tied what was left around my own waist. Thus we were secured to the mast and to each other. I slipped the short sword back into the sheath and hooked the small leather strip over the cross-bar.

My eyes searched for Fahda the Sun, and then I mentally worked out the direction in which Jorjos would be located, due East, in the opposite direction from which Fahda flew across the heavens. Then I turned to Illa, to find her staring seriously at me, her lips pursed, her eyes not quite frowning. The moment I turned, she looked away.

"What do you want, *Warrior?*" she demanded curtly. Her manner was that of one being caught stealing a Tal from the Temple basket.

"My name is Thoris, and I come from Rota!" I held back the sudden hurt from my voice. Her cold attitude seemed uncalled for.

"I remember your name quite well, *Warrior!*" she countered arrogantly.

I started to say something, then thought better of it. I had no idea what my mistake had been but realized that the manner of women was strange and the way of a Princess was even more mystifying.

I stared at Illa, marveled at her beauty, even when posed in such a superior manner. Her nose was upswept, delicate, her high cheek-bones fine, her flesh smooth, flawless, creamy. Those large green eyes burned at me like the jeweled gaze of a goddess staring with anger at her lowest subject.

When I did not reply and the silence had stiffened over like ice, she slowly looked away, as if fighting an inner war with herself.

"What is the matter?" I inquired, chagrined; for deep inside me had been a bursting joy at even being near her, and the thought of having so displeased this woman was all but unbearable. Still the injustice of her sudden anger hurt. "What have I done?"

"Warrior, Thoris of Rota, you forget that I am *princess,* and I wish you to remember that from now on!" She turned and glared directly at me. Oh, the fire and pride which flared in her lovely eyes!

"What have I done to...?"

"You have ordered me around like a common slave. I will give the orders now!" her lips set, determined, her eyes harshly challenged mine. Yet there was no real hint as to what she was thinking or feeling, for a complete screen isolated any suggestion of her real inner thoughts.

My own amazement at the sudden change was numbing. Until now I had been able to forget that this was the Princess of Haldolen. She had seemed simply a young woman, frightened, helpless, in great need of protection. Now without any warning she had become the haughty, royal daughter of our God-Lord Muda, conversing with a lowly Commoner, and though unable to avoid it, finding the experience obviously annoying.

"What would my Royal Princess wish?" It was impossible to keep the sarcasm from my voice. She was a Princess, but I had saved her life—and for that it seemed she owed me simple gratitude.

Her face turned sharply away. "Is there no way to get us to land?"

There was a light tremor in her voice, and I hesitated before answering.

"Well?"

"I imagine that if we attempted to...swim in *that* direction," I pointed to the East, in which we were drifting, "that in a couple of days we might be able to make it to Jorjos." Again my sarcasm transparent; I was immediately sorry for it.

Still all this time I was thinking fast, attempting to determine what little chance we might truly have to survive.

Princess Illa said something under her breath and fell silent. Then all at once her face unmasked from the harsh royal stone. She was once again the frightened human little girl. For a split second the expression lasted, then a veil fell once more over her face. Her features firmed, the full lips stiffened enough to control any suggestion of a tremble.

"Tell me honestly...Thoris of Rota, what are our chances? I so command you to speak the truth."

"Our chances...?" I mused thoughtfully, tempted to paint the real picture of certain death; but instead I lied. A deep study of her green eyes revealed stark, naked fear which no Royal Princess of Haldolen was supposed to reveal. I could not harden that fear into open, uncontrolled terror. "I have a plan which should get us to land much faster."

"Well?" With that single word she boldly revealed how greatly her morale had been uplifted by my statement. But again the veil shimmered and exposed the child behind the mask of royalty; the young girl turning to her protector with total conviction he could do the impossible.

How I wanted to reach out and pull her into my arms, comfort her, but I knew this was quite impossible. While my own experience with maidens was not completely limited, there was no doubt that Illa, Princess of all of Haldolen, was totally limited in her contact with men her own age, completely inexperienced for thus it has always been with a near-goddess.

"I'll swim in that direction. It will help—"

Much to my surprise Illa quickly announced: "It will be so! And if I, too, swim from my side, then we will make even faster progress, is that not so?"

All I could think of was the fact that even this idea was far-fetched, fantastic, a mere slim hope on transparent air. Yet if it would give Illa some real confidence in our survival, something to do and believe in, maybe it was for the best.

"It is so ordered!" she announced with finality before I could answer her.

I stared at Illa, amazed, for this was not the same woman who had spoken a few moments before. Princess Illa was surely a feline creature with great contrasts, startling surprises. Already she had revealed several different poses and attitudes: the helpless child, the angry haughty princess, the companion willing to do her part to fight our way out of

26

this hopeless situation. One could not wish more from a male companion—other than greater strength. I was speechless with wonder. It was quite impossible to understand this woman, this Princess whom I so totally loved.

"Well?" Illa demanded. "Don't stare at me. Let's begin!"

Immediately I turned and pushed away from the mast, until I was the full length of the rope, about five heads. I tread water.

Illa's voice called: "Are you ready?"

"Yes."

As I began to swim my heart burned with pride at the thought of Illa's bravery, strength and character.

At first it looked like we were wasting our time, for the mast seemed unwilling to move any faster. But slowly our speed built.

How long could we continue swimming till exhaustion overtook us? And even if we could keep it up all day and night, would it make any real difference? I could hardly believe that. Yet it was far better than merely waiting to die without even trying. It was this or nothing. Exhaustion would finally cause the Princess Illa to fall asleep, and maybe that was for the good.

As I swam I thought about how beautiful the ocean is when viewed from the shore, seeming to stretch out to infinity—at least to the very end of the world. How many times I looked out to sea as a child and wondered how far it really stretched. But nobody knows for sure the extent of our world. I had pondered the theory of Lorndas many times as a child. He who believes, as all students know, that the world might be a cylinder. But that one could go in one direction— to East or West as Lorndas suggests—and finally, after many Seasons, return to the same place they began, seems incredible if not outright impossible. The theory that cold lands of the North and South blend down into the Pits of Ice upon which our world exists is far more logical.

But now the ocean as seen from the surface defied all beauty and certainly limited my ability to theorize about it or the world, or all that God Fahda created. We were surrounded by cold, bottomless waters. We continued to swim, and each stroke seemed to have no other effect than to further exhaust our muscles. Certainly there was no sign of progress of any kind; none, like on the land where one will pass brush, a hill, travel over a mountain. Here watery hills and mountains moved at will, waving all around us.

I remember marveling at Illa's strength and great ability to swim for such a long time. But as Fahda sank into the western ocean, I heard her gasp, and pull herself half across the mast. Her eyes were glazed as they stared at me.

Immediately I swam close, took hold of Illa's arms, pulled the rope tighter to the mast, then arranged her body in such a manner that it would be possible for her to remain supported even while sleeping.

During all this she said nothing. When I was finished she merely closed her eyes.

I stayed close, holding to the mast with my right arm, the water up to my shoulders.

My eyes ran the length of her face, took in the soft hollows of her throat, white and smooth, lightly beating. Her shoulders and back were covered in the light weight tuda—the one-piece gown that slipped over the head, resting on the shoulders, which was quite popular at the time. A harsh lump formed in my throat as I thought of her long struggle against the ocean, attempting to help move the mast forward.

Then darkness slipped upon the world and the stars twinkled against the sky, and finally Lonu the Moon passed into the heavens; half her pale face showed to light the calmed water of the Haldolen Ocean.

The moonlight caressed soft strokes of cream across Illa's even, smooth features. For a long, long time I continued to keep faithful watch over the Princess. But the rhythm of the mast moving gently up and down with the rocking waves, the pale cast of the moonlight as it streaked across the waters, and the exhaustion which had already weakened the muscles of my body, all blended together to gently numb my mind into a deep slumber.

How long I was unconscious I do not really know. Maybe a moment, maybe a very long time. How I managed to keep from submerging I will never know. Which gods watched over Illa while sleep stole away my watchfulness, I can only bless and thank.

The next thing I knew was hearing the distant murmur of breaking waves as they splashed against a beach. At first it seemed I was dreaming. I did not move, but simply lay there, almost completely covered by water, listening to the distant surf.

I opened my eyes, as if that would help my hearing, and gazed out toward the East. Every sense attempted to seek out some indication of lands but only misty haze pressed in from all sides. It was difficult even to see the end of the mast, where it floated on the surface of the ocean.

I continued to listen for some time as the noise grew louder and more distinct.

"What is it?" Illa whispered, suddenly.

"Waves hitting a beach—but it can't be!"

"Land!" her face lighted with bright fires, hope made a large smile that generously revealed even white teeth. "Land."

"Quiet!"

"Don't tell me what to do!" Princess Illa commanded, hotly.

"Quiet!" Surprisingly she didn't say another word.

We seemed to be moving faster than before. The ocean pounding against the beach was now louder, clearer; explosions which resounded throughout the night air. I felt the responding beat of my heart as it reacted with sudden excitement—and hope! For the first time since being swept into the water it was possible to believe that we might live.

"Come! Swim!" I pushed away from the mast and started to kick toward the sound of the unknown beach. Strength now surged into being; hope had given me reason to continue, to fight for life.

I heard Illa swimming on the other side of the mast and felt a sense of pride that she had overcome her natural instinct to refuse orders from a common warrior.

We moved faster through the water, gaining speed; the current helped to push us forward. Then as I realized we were closer to shore than it had seemed at the beginning, I stopped, called to Illa.

"Untie yourself. We can swim without the mast from here on! The mast will be dangerous when we hit the waves!" All the time I worked the loop from around my own body. I finally threw it from me. "How're you coming?"

"It's off," Illa called back.

I ducked under the water and swam beyond the mast to Illa's side. As I surfaced within arm's reach of the Princess, she gasped in surprise.

"Come! Follow me." I started swimming once more, after having pushed the mast away from us. I kept Illa within easy reach. If she needed help of any kind I would be there instantly.

For the first time I realized how icy the water had become. My flesh was numbed. Now with the mast already out of sight in the thickening mists, I could not help but wonder how wise it had been to cut away from it. What if the surf was beyond our ability to reach it in time?

"Are you all right?" I called, hiding the sense of looming fear from my voice.

"I'm fine." But her voice was tired, strained.

"Here, let me help you!" I reached for her.

"No!" That word shot out like the clash of metal on metal. "I'm *fine.*"

The beach was already closer. The water rolled more powerfully, as if building to the crushing size of tidal waves in order to break upon a sandy or rocky beach. Then waves rose around us much higher than before and for a moment it seemed we were about to be plunged into the crown of a great rippling crest. But the water lapped down again into a deep valley.

The sound of the surf was explosive now, almost on top of us. My mind was picturing all sorts of rugged, dangerous shorelines of rock or cliffs which would slice out from the ocean floor to loom ominously above like giants of destruction and death.

Then the water under us reared higher than ever, and I saw ahead of us, through the mists, tall, dark, menacing shadows, and believed the worst.

The water rumbled, exploded under us. Desperately I reached for Illa but she was too far away.

Then the wave swiftly rushed forward, carrying me with it. I felt the water churn, then buckle under with horrifying force. The roar of the ocean seemed like the screaming voices of all the ocean gods of Naypean taunting us to our last resting place of death.

Then I was sucked under the water and tumbled over and over under the strong impact of the brutal wave as it charged rapidly toward the shore. My only thought was for Illa's safety but it was impossible to succor her. She might already be dead. How could such a frail woman possibly survive what had me totally powerless?

Then the breath was slammed out of my lungs as I was smashed downwards to hit the sandy beach. The wave pushed me forward at amazing speed. I was only half-conscious as the waters receded, leaving me deposited on the damp pebbly beach.

CHAPTER THREE

TERROR ON TAGOR

Blackness was like a frozen hand clutching around my brain and thoughts. Consciousness slipped and I lay in the dimensionless world where even dreams have no being. Then I heard the sound of Illa's voice just above me.

"Are you all right? Thoris, are you all right?" There was a frantic pleading in her voice, as if the very thought that something serious might have happened to me was too much to bear. "Thoris. Thoris! Tell me you're all right!"

I opened my eyes and saw the dark form of Illa's head leaning over me. I could not see the expression on her features because of the misty dark of night pressing around us.

"Are *you* all right?" I managed weakly.

A long silence answered me. Then Illa finally said, in a totally controlled, formal voice: "Yes. I'm fine. I thought maybe you were...hurt!"

I didn't move, simply lay there silently looking up into that oval face which was too darkened to really see. But it was enough to have her close. It would have been so easy to reach up and pull her down into my arms. The temptation was almost overpowering. I knew she would be quite defenseless against the strength of my arms. And who was to punish me? I doubted very much that we would ever return to Haldolen—where punishment for so touching the daughter of Muda would have been slow, painful death at the hands of her father's Temple priests.

The shape of her body silhouetted against the lighter background of the sky taunted my passions. She was all too

32

near, all too helpless. And it was this last, among so many other things, which controlled me. Her very helplessness was her protection. I could never do anything to harm her, then or ever.

"How long was I unconscious?"

For a moment she did not answer. Her voice, when she spoke, was hesitant, soft: "Only a short while. I was washed upon the shore not far from you. I must have been lucky and missed the full power of the wave."

I sat up. "You're not hurt?"

"No. Not that I know of." She slipped away just beyond arm's reach.

"The Gods are kind."

"Yes," she murmured.

We sat there for some time without speaking. I was aware of the cold of the night and the wetness which still enveloped my body.

I surveyed our surroundings. There was a small beach which stopped short before a huge forest.

"Wait here," I instructed, standing, drawing my short sword and starting toward the trees.

"Where are you going?" Illa sounded frightened.

"I'll be right back. You'll be safe. I'll keep you in sight."

"What are you doing? I command you!" Illa shouted. "Answer me."

I slipped into the forest without responding. The trees were thickly grown together even here, and the underbrush just thin enough to make it quite impossible for me to be seen. I turned to look at Illa, and felt like some kind of evil fiend, peeking through the foliage upon my Princess while she bathed in the perfumed baths of the Temple of Muda. A hot flush raced through my body, burned my cheeks.

I turned and started to search for firewood. It did not take long for the forest was fertile with plenty of dried wood and leaves. I even saw a few fruit trees and picked a couple of ripe juicy apples.

As I returned to shore, Illa sat facing the ocean. She did not move at my approach. But when I leaned over to deposit the wood behind and a little to her left, she whipped angrily around.

"Warrior! How dare you ignore your Princess." Her eyes blazed. "I gave you a direct..."

But she had already seen and focused on the apples in my hands and the words faded out. Hunger defeated royal anger. Her lips hung open. She seemed to lean slightly forward as if unable to control this outward sign of the great need her body felt for good food.

"Here, catch!" I tossed one of the apples to her. It was not the princely thing to do but after all I was merely a common warrior and felt something inside me that urged me to make her realize that no matter how royal she was, in my eyes she was also a human woman—not solely a goddess. I wanted to forget that she was anything other than a beautiful woman. A woman who might be mine someday. A fantasy dream—but better than the cruel reality which placed her far beyond my reach! For more terrible was the fact she would probably be dead within a few days. What a waste of womanly beauty her death would be!

A pleasant sense of total power and gratification came to me as she caught the fruit with the grace of a dainty bird swooping down from the skies to snatch up some morsel of food in midair.

Without any formality. Illa grabbed the apple with both hands and took a large hungry bite from it. Then immediately her attitude changed. She began to masticate more slowly, taking her time, giving dignity to her actions. The control was magnificent! For hunger had reduced both of us to a state of savage animals.

I finished off my apple and threw the core out to sea. Bending over, I started arranging the firewood and leaves so they would catch flame more quickly. I then reached inside my harness pouch and pulled out a flint and striking stone. In a short time a small fire blazed brightly.

Both of us huddled around the glowing flames, warming our hands and bodies. Illa had said nothing since eating the fruit but her eyes had been on me most of the time. When I'd look up she would quickly turn away.

"You must be very tired, why don't you rest?" I suggested. I was already sorry for my earlier rudeness. "I'll keep watch."

She started to say something, then looked away; ignored me. A little later she suddenly blurted out, as if it were her own idea:

"You know, *Warrior,* I think I'll rest. You, *Warrior,* will keep guard over me!"

With that she curled up next to the fire and closed her eyes.

I leaned closer to the flames and felt their warmth reach up and surge through my body. The chill of the ocean was slowly slipping away and now only cold night penetrated my nerves.

I looked down at Princess Illa and wondered what fate was in store for her. She was such a delicate, proud woman. All her life she had been surrounded by the softness of the Royal Temple of Muda and the Warriors of her father's personal court. Now alone with a strange warrior from Rota, she must face unknown adventures which might end in horrible death.

For a long time my eyes watched over her, until the even falling and rising of her breast revealed that she was asleep. Bewildering emotions surged through me as I looked upon her. She was so beautiful. The softness of her long blond hair, now almost dry, flowed over her shoulders. The flickering flames cast highlights over her smooth features, the upturned pout of her full red lips, the roundness of her large eyes, the gentle sweep of her smooth throat, pale as pinkest porcelain; the soft slenderness of her arms and body.

My complete attention was so fully on Illa that I don't know what made me look up at that moment. Maybe some inner awareness. It was something not heard or felt but that which silently pressed out from the darkness to announce itself to my nerves.

Abruptly my senses were alert. The cells of my body tingled, the muscles hardened. My right hand fairly leapt for the short sword, unlatched the leather band which held it in place.

Something was behind me.

I listened, then jumped to my feet, whirled. The short sword slammed into my hand, whipped free of the sheath, shot out in one downward stroke.

There was no hint of what might be threatening me. I had no idea what to expect but merely acted, letting my instinct take control. My muscles went into action without questioning what kind of possible danger might lurk behind me.

The blade of my sword sank into the skull of a savage, an all but naked warrior, who was carrying a long, deadly-looking spear. Immediately behind him were a half a dozen others who quickly surged forward. Spears threatened me like sword points. The warrior slumped to the ground in a dead heap as his fellow leaped forward to take his place.

I parried one spear thrust, leaped in and struck another weapon, slicing it in two pieces. Then my sword moved from left to right, nicking an arm, cutting into the neck of a third savage.

My first impression of these men was one of horror, for their faces were gaunt, the eyes deep-set in their sockets, the lips thin, pulled tight over sharp pointed teeth which exposed themselves as low growls uttered from the corded thin throats. They seemed like walking men of death. Hair, long and black, fell like matted strings around their shoulders. They wore g-straps around their middles, made of what appeared to be soft animal hides—and later proved such. They were beardless and their flesh seemed pale and sickly even in the darkness of night.

"Princess Illa! Illa! Run!" I shouted over my shoulder as my short sword flashed out in a brutal series of viscous attacks meant to keep the savages back as long as possible. Time was not on my side. Had I possessed a long sword things might have been different. But the short sword, hardly longer than a man's forearm and hand extended out straight, was a disadvantage against the thrusts of long spears.

I felt a couple of jabs of pain as the tips of the savages' spears just touched me, drawing blood. How I escaped death is beyond my ability to guess.

I now attacked, leaping into their ranks, hacking madly from left to right, thrusting, cutting down as many as

36

possible. My blade sank into a stomach, pulled out bloody and then flew across a naked chest, cutting through flesh and ribs. Then suddenly I felt something hard hit the back of my head. My right arm swung, attempted to strike at the opponent in front of me. But the man grinned toothily and struck the sword from my grasp with his spear as I fell forward.

My face hit the pebbly beach and then I heard a scream and knew they had also taken Princess Illa. My last thought was realization of total defeat: it would have been far better if Princess Illa had drowned rather than face what must now be in store for her.

* * * * * * *

Blind pain came first. Then it started to take form and finally gain a rhythm which became quite annoying. It was if some fiendish creature from the pits of the dead were greedily sucking on the back of my skull in an attempt to withdraw my life force. I thought to attempt to strike it off but could not move.

My thoughts were blurred for a long time. It was hard to remember what had happened last. Everything seemed distant and faraway. Then memory of the storm flooded back and at first I believed I was still in the water.

A moan sounded from beside me.

Muscles moved, tested their strength, relaxed. All at once I remembered being washed ashore, gathering firewood, being attacked.

My eyes snapped open. I turned.

I was lying on the dirt floor of a crude mud hut, which had only one opening, just large enough for a man to step through. Light flooded into the small confines of the dwelling. Almost immediately upon sitting up, I saw Illa lying next to me. She was asleep. my first instinct was to awaken her, then I reconsidered. Instead, I turned my attention to the entrance of the hut.

The view was limited but I could make out several other huts and saw men, women and children moving around outside. The women were engaged in various duties: preparing food, weaving, carrying water and the like. The naked children ran around chasing each other in laughing play. The men worked with stones, sharpened spears, or sat around talking among themselves.

Just beyond the farthest hut I could make out a strange tall pole which had been carved in astonishing design, showing painted angry faces of men and women. Beyond that was the forest. The sound of birds mingled with the laughter of playing children and conversation of men and women.

It all seemed quite natural. This was a primitive tribe which had not learned the ways of civilization. There were few places where the culture of Haldolen had not touched within such a short distance from its shore.

The men were gaunt, their bodies but bones with muscles stretched thinly over them, with pale, sickly flesh to make a covering. Still there was normalcy about this scene which I gazed upon. It could have been, in a primitive form, any family gathering of Haldolen.

Illa stirred. I turned and saw her slowly sit up. There was a puzzled expression on her face. Then a soft moan of despair trembled pitifully past those lovely, dimpled red lips.

I wanted to reach out and comfort her, but controlled the foolish urge.

"Where are we?" She gazed through the opening in the small hut. "What are they going to do with us?"

"I thought maybe you might know."

"I passed out when they captured me."

"Why didn't you run, as instructed?"

"I couldn't leave you there, alone," she stated as if it were the most logical and obvious thing in the world for a Princess to remain to be captured while her slave-warrior attempted to make her escape possible.

Then she added more emotionally: "And anyway, I am not your slave to do as you tell me to do!"

"I was willing to die to give you a chance to get away!" I exploded, making no attempt to hold back my angry shock.

She grew rigid and for a moment I felt the heat of her eyes blazing at me. "How dare you question my actions!"

38

"What could you have done, anyway?" I felt a deep sense of bitterness attack me. I wanted so much to protect my Princess and yet everything I had done so far had led to complete disaster.

"Where would I have gone without..." She hesitated, then continued in a forceful tone of voice: "Without a warrior I would be helpless in the ocean or in the jungles or forest or mountains. I did not believe we would be captured, anyway! I thought I was safe, with you to protect me. Any other warrior would have died rather than be captured—he'd be dead...and I'd be here alone—and that is the way of a great warrior of my people!"

"And there would be nobody to protect you in the future if the warrior had died. At least there is some hope— with me alive, though captured!" I pointed out a little annoyed, but also amused by her lack of logic which had tripped her up.

She shrugged as if what I had said meant nothing. "How was I to know you could not fight off those savages? The Great Thoris of Rota, great warrior—hah!"

With that Illa turned away, and as far as she was concerned I did not exist.

I sat staring at her. My mind formed bitter replies. But instead of speaking I remained silent.

My thoughts wandered over the events which had lead us to our captivity, a series of tragic disasters that had been completely beyond my poor ability to control.. Yet, we were still alive! We were breathing, and maybe there was still hope. Captured though we were, it might be possible to escape. With escape, maybe we would have a chance to find a haven of safety. My thoughts actually did not go much beyond that—for who knows what the Gods might have in store beyond the next hill, around the next curve in the path?

I stood, stretched, and then stepped over to the opening. My actions were casual but all nerves and muscles tensely alert. I was merely curious as to how far I might continue without being stopped. There did not seem to be any guard at the entrance.

I got to the opening, my head just leaned out when suddenly I was facing an armed guard who had been posted to the left of the entrance, beyond our sight.

"Back!" the man growled, thrusting with the pointed spear.

"Where are we?" I inquired conversationally, not moving.

"Tagor. The Isle of Tagor!" The spear pressed at my naked chest. "Back!"

"Say, what are you fellows going to do with us?" I edged away from the spear, moving farther into the hut, but still on the surface friendly and casual.

The fellow grinned, revealing sharp points of his teeth, which looked more like fangs. "You will see soon enough!"

"What about food?" I pointed to Illa. "She is hungry and thirsty."

The man grinned more broadly. "Food is scarce. But I will have some of the women bring fruit. That will satisfy your thirst and hunger all at once. After all, we don't want you growing too thin. You must be plump, juicy!" With that the man laughed loudly. It was a high crackling sound that vibrated from his scrawny neck. Then he disappeared from view.

I turned, stared at Illa, wondered if she had guessed the meaning of his last words and the laughter. A shudder was silently tingling down my spine at what my mind was conjuring up.

Her face was pale, lips compressed into thin white lines. For a moment she stared up at me, wide-eyed.

"We'll escape!" I assured her in a whisper.

But Illa did not answer. She just sat there, hands in her lap, looking up at me with sick terror glazing over her eyes.

"Illa! Snap out of it!" I slipped down beside her. "Snap out of it. This isn't the time to go into shock!"

Then I reached out and grabbed her shoulders. It was as if lightning had struck the hut. Illa all at once jerked, then violently yanked away. Her eyes closed, hands went up to

40

cover her face. For a moment she did not move, then slowly her soft white shoulders shook.

I sat there unable to do anything, afraid to touch her for fear of her reaction. My shock at the physical contact had welled a wild electric sensation through me which was almost overwhelming. I was still weak from the reaction of surprise.

Illa lowered her hands and slowly turned. "I'm sorry."

Her voice was firm but soft. "We must leave this place, of course." Her eyes were wide, innocent; they held the blind faith of a child toward a Great Wizard or one of the many lesser Gods, knowing that somehow the impossible can happen. "You will find a way? You will take me out of this ugly place?"

For a long moment I sat there unable to speak. She looked up at me much like that little child expecting a wonderful, fantastic magic from the Learned Wizard. It was almost as if she were talking about going on a walk to the ocean for the afternoon.

"Well?" she persisted. "I am waiting your answer."

"Well, Princess..." I frantically sought to find words but they lay beyond my reach. How could I tell her that I was not a miracle maker and that there was actually little chance of us ever leaving this village or island alive? And even escaping the village would probably only mean recapture. Unless we could find a way to escape the island itself, all efforts would end up just about the same. "I...I am working out some plan. Just give me a little time," I finally managed to ad lib.

"Fine! I will await your announcement with eagerness!" She clasped her hands on her lap and sat there, staring eagerly at me.

"It might take a little time."

"I am in no hurry. I don't believe I'm going any place until you think of something. Do you?" She smiled, pleased with herself, and it was difficult to tell is she was attempting some sardonic humor at my expense—mocking, teasing—or merely felt so hopeless that it was impossible to be totally oblivious to any form of hope, no matter how small.

I wasn't really sure if she were laughing at me or quite serious and so found it impossible to formulate any reply which would reflect her true meaning. But there was no time to worry about that for at that moment the sound of footsteps came from outside, then voices.

"He's for you to guard, too."

"Another feast? The Gods have been kind. We will have a grand celebration!" That was the voice of our jailor.

Then the warrior appeared, his spear pointed at the back of another man, dressed much as himself. "In there, with the others!"

The prisoner stepped into the hut, looked at me, then sat down against the far wall, glancing at Illa for one long moment before dropping his gaze to the ground.

For a while nobody said anything. Then I finally broke the silence.

"I am Thoris and this is...Illa." I had almost said "Princess" and then thought better of it. "What is your name?"

The man looked up at me, then said: "Tekop."

"Why are you a prisoner?"

"I am from Suruas-Tagor—across on the other side of the Isle of Tagor. I was hunting when men of Hua-Tagor captured me. They are planning a great celebration and feast in honor of the Chief's daughter's union with a warrior. So...they are hunting for meats for the feast."

Tekop sounded so casual that I wondered if I had guessed right about our fate.

"What exactly are they going to do with us?"

"You do not know?" The other man's mouth was wide with amazement. The deep-set eyes blinked a couple of times.

"We are from faraway—across the water," I explained. "We were washed ashore last night by the storm. We know nothing of Tagor."

The man studied us both more carefully. "Yes..." he said thoughtfully, "I see it now. You are probably from Jorjos—or the lands beyond the ocean—I believe the Ijans call it Haldolen. Since you wear such strange clothing I would guess the latter. But..." He shrugged. "It doesn't matter from where you come. You will go to the same place for which I am destined: into the stomachs of the Hua-Tagor."

Illa's gasp of shock was pitiful. I felt a churning sickness of my own eat painfully at the lining of my stomach. My first guess had been all too correct.

"You mean they eat *humans?*" Illa cried in a high-pitched voice.

"Why, of course! Is there any other food fit for true warriors? Only women and children will eat the fruits of the forest and grow weak and fat. *Men* eat flesh."

"But surely the animals—" I started to suggest, but he interrupted.

"Animals are better than nothing." Tekop admitted. "But there is nothing to replace the meat of man. And best of all is the flesh of those who have just died in slow agony, for their muscles are hardened, their blood more—"

"Please—I understand!" I glanced at Illa, who was now covering her mouth in horror.

The Sasuas-Tagor laughed. "You do not do the same where you come from?"

"Of course not!" I fairly yelled in disgust. "We are *civilized.*" I had to fight the inner anger burning in my gut. This man was an insane fool.

"What *do* you eat?" The island savage looked honestly puzzled. At least the grinning had momentarily stopped. "You are strong looking. I would think you are a mighty warrior. Where do you get your strength from if not from the flesh and muscle and blood of man?"

"The meat of animals. The fruits of the trees and the roots of plants."

"What do you do with your dead?" Tekop leaned forward, deep interest tensing his ugly, sunken features.

"With our dead?" I could not quite believe the implied meaning.

"Yes, with your dead? Do you not eat them?"

It was Illa who spoke then. Her voice was strangely strong, level. "You mean you eat your dead?"

"Why, of course," he announced matter-of-factly, as if it were the most natural thing in the world. "What better means of disposing of dead bodies? To let them rot and be fed upon by the animals of the forest is a waste of good flesh. Surely you do not do such a ghastly thing?" The man shuddered visibly. He recoiled against the wall of the hut, as if in horror at the very thought of what we had suggested.

"We bury them," I explained. "Bury them so that they may rest in peace, untouched by other than the Gods. For they are the only ones who have the right to eat of the dead."

The man's deep-set eyes blinked. For a moment his lips hung open, then snapped loudly closed. Finally he gasped out, "But...you *waste* food! What a terrible loss. You come from an insane land where healthy food is thrown away! And you call *that* civilized?"

"But then it is said that those of Jorjos are much the same...come to think of it. I—"

"I believe that is quite enough!" Princess Illa announced in her most regal tone of command.

Tekop's eyes snapped to Illa. "Silence, woman!"

Illa looked as if she had been slapped. "How dare you speak to me in that manner. I am—"

I interjected: "Illa—please!"

Those eyes fired raw, then suddenly simmered down as she saw the hard, warning expression on my face.

I turned to Tekop. "I am afraid you have frightened her by your words."

"*I* frightened her?" Tekop sounded astounded. "But it is *your* words that horrify *me!* Disgust me! How one could dare waste such good food thus is beyond me. It's sinful. Oh...when it is so scarce!" he looked away, shaking his head from side to side like a man who just cannot accept what he has heard as truth. "It is true then, what I've heard about the insane ones. Those across the waters!" He was talking to himself, eyes glazed, distant. "I did not believe the rumors."

For a moment I said nothing. Then, when the silence seemed oppressive, I asked: "When does this...well...feast take place?"

He looked up eagerly, his mood immediately brightening. "Two days from now. I heard them talking as they brought me up here."

"We must find a means of escape."

"They will never give you the chance."

"I don't plan on asking."

"Believe me, there is no way to escape. In my village, as in this one, you would be killed immediately upon attempting to leave. And...even if you did escape, where would you go that they could not track you? For we Tagors are great trackers." The last he said in great pride, expanding his chest, grinning like some mindless moron.

"But we must try," I persisted.

"Yes, Thoris of Rota will think of something," Princess Illa declared in a voice filled with pride. "For he is a great warrior and there is nothing he cannot do."

I shifted my gaze from her to Tekop and back to the Princess. From one extreme to the other she had leaped. She seemed to have complete blind faith in me; and the Tagorian had none at all.

It was the last statement anybody made for a long time, as if it were enough. I sat there thinking, trying hard to discover some plan that might promise us freedom. But the longer I thought the more convinced I became that it was hopeless. We were surrounded by the enemy, fully armed and willing to use weapons to bring our lives to an immediate end. And even if we were to leave the village, as Tekop suggested, we would be tracked down and killed. Though, of course, this might be more merciful for Illa, since our deaths, according to Tekop, were not to be quick ones.

But even after fruit was brought for us, my thoughts were completely devoid of any plan of escape. Death surely seemed to lurk in the immediate future and there was nothing I could do to prevent it.

CHAPTER FOUR

THE TREACHERY OF TEKOP

Night settled upon the world, and cook-fires burned dimly in front of the small huts, creating an eerie glow that flickered on the savage, primitive village. The night was warm, for the Season of Summer still prevailed; even so, it seemed cold in the hut.

Illa was sleeping. Tekop still sat opposite us. He had hardly stopped watching me. It was as if he were trying to solve some illusive puzzle. Possibly he could not decide if we were to be considered friends or enemies, regardless of the fact that all three of us were fellow captives.

As I sat there in the hut, my thoughts ran over and over all possibilities of escape. Then a desperate idea re-suggested itself.

The inescapable fact was that no matter what we did there was a good chance we would be killed. In an escape attempt it might be a fast death—and there was always the chance that we might pull it off. The fact that there was nothing to lose forced me to the conclusion that the sooner we began the better it would be.

Once I considered my plan it seemed all too simple and obvious. Of course, the thought had occurred to me before, at the very beginning, but had been rejected at first as too risky.

"Tekop," I whispered after slipping closer to the Tagorian, who was by now almost asleep. I stopped within whispering distance.

The man's head swung toward me. "Yes?"

"Quiet!" I warned. "If I convince you there is a means of escaping, would you want to go with us?" I spoke in a very low voice so that the guards outside might not hear. The conversation that followed was all in whispers.

"Of course. Nobody wants to go into the guts of another warrior. But there is no way to escape."

"There's *one*. It's risky. But what choice do we have?" I silently considered the man, then continued: "Is there a way off the island?"

"Why?" he asked defensively.

"Because I don't believe that Illa nor myself will be welcomed on the island. Would your people welcome us with open arms?"

"I see what you mean. They would capture you and you would feed the bellies of the Sasuas-Tagor rather than the Hua-Tagor. You are quite right. So—why bother to even attempt escape?" The man shrugged, then grinned. It was obvious from the pleased expression on his sickly face that he believed this would surely end the subject.

"Is there some way off the island?" I leaned closer and gazed into his sallow, haggard features.

"Yes—but it could be dangerous!" He looked suddenly uncomfortable, as if some disquieting thought had occurred to him.

"How?"

"By small-boat. But on the ocean...what chance would one have? We have many such small boasts for fishing, exploring and sporting. The Sasuas-Tagor are great sportsmen. The Hua-Tagor attempt to follow our lead but they never were great hunters or fishermen. We of the Sasuas-Tagor are the greatest hunters in all the world—so how could men of this tribe be half as good?" He spat on the floor in front of him.

"But is it possible to get a small-boat?" I demanded, irritated by his side-tracking. "I would need a boat to get Illa and myself off the island."

"It could be arranged," Tekop admitted. "But what kind of plan do you have?"

"First, tell me, what's behind this hut?"

"Nothing—just the forest. I came into the village from that direction."

"Just as I imagined from the layout of the village I have seen from the opening of our hut. Then we can dig ourselves out and go into the forest." I felt a sudden surge of relief.

Tekop stared at me and then his lips opened, spread wide until I could see the yellow-stained pointed teeth as he laughed uncontrollably.

I didn't say anything until he had finished with his hysterics. The amazing thing was that one of the guards outside near the camp fire did not wonder what was going on and investigate. Finally, Tekop sobered, said: "You must be joking."

"Why not? What's wrong with the idea?"

The man looked puzzled, his features squeezed tightly together. Then having considered my question for some time, he nodded. "Why not? You are quite right, there is no reason we could not dig ourselves out. But then what?"

"In darkness we go into the forest and..."

"But the forest has many night-creatures who are hungry for the flesh of man!" Tekop shuddered, shook his head from side to side. "It would be quite impossible."

"It would not be any more deadly than staying here, waiting to die," I pointed out.

"You are right. Quite right. It wouldn't be any more dangerous, come to think of it." He nodded his head up and down like the bobbing of a galley in a stormy sea.

"We dig under the wall of the hut, then slip out the other side."

"They will hear us," Tekop warned.

"Why should they if we are silent? They are sitting around the fire to keep warm—that is far enough away...if we are quiet in our work!"

Tekop thought for a moment. "Why not just call one of the guards and kill him? We would then be armed and have a much better chance of escaping."

"No—I considered that. There are too many guards at the camp fire. They might see us. As you said, this hut faces the forest."

"Yes...you are quite right again." He was thoughtful. His face finally brightened. "I believe you have hit on a truly workable plan. Why nobody has ever thought of it before is beyond me. But then...nobody ever attempts to escape once they are captured. Capture is defeat. Defeat does not make one think of turning it into victory by escaping!"

"Well, let's begin!" I pointed to the opposite side of the hut, but a body's length away. "Over there!"

"A little to the right," Tekop announced, making his way to the place he indicated. "If we dig here it should not be long until we can be out in the forest."

I turned, crept over to Princess Illa and placed a hand gently over her mouth.

She jerked awake; her eyes snapped open, frightened. Muffled sounds came from her lips.

While releasing her, I explained my plan, ending with: "You keep watch and give us any warning if the guards get up."

Illa's face flushed, and resentment fired those lovely green eyes; but she nodded and slipped over to where Tekop had been sitting before, so that she had a good position to be forewarned if any guard started to get up and come to the hut.

Then I moved to Tekop's side, ripped the oval rank-marker from the front of my harness strap; it was made of hard metal which would serve wonderfully to help us dig into the soft ground.

Right from the start it appeared a good-size job. Not only did we have to dig but also had to displace the dirt, spreading it out on the floor in such a way that it would not be obviously visible to anybody immediately looking into the hut.

At one time a guard stood, and Illa hissed us to silence. The two of us lay down on the dirt, hiding our efforts, as if asleep. Then apparently the guard went back to the camp fire. For a long while nobody moved. Then when it seemed quite safe, I sat up, and once more began digging.

After that there was no rest, for both of us believed that if we did not finish in the night and leave before morning, there would never be another chance.

I must admit some surprise at Tekop's enthusiasm once he began. It seemed as if the minute he was convinced there was hope, no task was too difficult or tiring. Scrawny as his body appeared, it moved with grace and amazing speed, pushing aside dirt as I piled it up. And all this in almost total silence.

Halfway through we met with disappointment. We had already dug a portion wide enough to allow the passage of a man and had begun to work under the wall itself. We now came to a wooden staff about the thickness of a man's wrist.

Tekop whispered: "Framework which supports the hut. I was afraid of that. We have to dig around it. The posts are wide enough apart to make passage between them quite possible."

It was a delay which ate up a lot of time and energy. But finally we managed to dig around it, pushing the earth to one side, not even bothering to spread it around the floor. Once beyond the wall we managed to keep from breaking the surface, leaving a thin roof of dirt to hide our efforts from the outside, in case somebody happened to pass by.

The first suggestion of a chill morning, the hint of Fahda the Sun coming awake, was already upon us as we completed our work.

I silently motioned to Illa then slipped into the shallow hole we had dug and worked my way under the wall, just barely squeezing through. I pushed up with my head, using all the strength of every muscle. We had worked almost to the surface, so it was, in reality, a simple matter to shove through the small layer of dirt which remained. Yet for what seemed an eternity I strained against the dirt. The hurried labor of the night had already told on my strength. Then suddenly my head felt the earth above give away. Almost immediately I was covered with dirt. Sputtering, shaking my head, I managed to worm upward. It was a long struggle, for the confines of our little escape tunnel was quite cramped.

All this time fear of discovery haunted me. I half expected to find myself facing a grim-faced armed guard. But luck or the Gods were with us. Every moment, every action had been done as silently as humanly possible. Finally I pulled myself out of the narrow, small tunnel under the hut wall. I stood, thanking the Gods.

I dug the loose dirt away, then waited almost breathlessly. There was the soft murmur of confusion from inside the hut. Then suddenly everything was quiet. I saw a form work its way past the wall. A moment later the head of Tekop poked into sight. Angrily I yanked him out. There wasn't time to argue the point that Illa should have come out first.

Illa started through the tunnel. I saw her head first, then shoulders, then gently I helped her crawl the rest of the way out and pulled her to her feet.

Without a word we headed toward the dark, foreboding forest.

I kept close to Illa, right behind Tekop, whom I had allowed to take the lead, since he knew his way around the island.

It was some time before any of us spoke, and only then after we reached a clearing, beyond which showed the ocean of Haldolen. Fahda the Sun was already beginning to peek over the eastern horizon to dimly light the sky and water in morning orange.

I called a stop to our progress and the three of us huddled together.

"We have to find a boat!" I instructed Tekop.

"There is none here," he announced as if giving me information that was totally new.

"But where?"

"Near my village, on the other side of the island," he said, looking from me to Illa.

"What about going back and getting one of the Hua-Tagor's boats?" Something worried me about the man's attitude. He was too evasive.

"But they will soon be after us. We cannot take the chance!" Tekop insisted much too angrily.

I stared at him for a moment before saying: "I'm going back. You tell me where the boats are. We will have a better chance on the water. They will not be able to track us then."

He started to object, then shrugged. "That way."

He pointed back along the shore, to the right. "They should have them hidden in the brushes somewhere along the shore."

I turned in that direction. It was a mistake.

Almost immediately a cry of alarm came from Illa.

Before I could do much more than tense a muscle. I felt the impact of a body slam into my back. At first I could not even guess what was attacking me. Then I fell to the ground and saw a thin, pale hand reach for my throat.

There wasn't any time to consider why Tekop had jumped me.

Before I could do anything to defend myself I felt the impact of something hard hit my head. I recoiled, dazed. Tekop's knee slammed up into my groin. The world burst into agonizing pain.

I heard a frightened scream, but everything was distant, faraway, as if experienced in some hellish nightmare, created by a Wizard's evil spell.

I tried to move, attempted to recover from the searing torture that now enveloped me. But all I could do was double over, writhe in the world of red haze.

"Thoris! *Thoris!*" Illa's voice screamed.

"Quiet, woman! Let the Hua-Tagors have him! And they will have you, too, if you do not come quietly with me. I'll kill you!" Tekop's voice threatened from the distant world I could not reach.

"Kill me then!" was Illa's brave reply.

"You come with me!" Tekop announced. There was a sound of something hard hitting soft flesh, followed by a soft moan.

I fought to open my eyes. It seemed to take forever, then suddenly I was looking upon a scene that filled me with such rage that the strength seethed through my now quivering muscles.

Tekop was lifting the unconscious form of Princes Illa into his arms.

"Tekop!" I managed to scream through the agony which still gnawed cruelly at my groin.

The other turned, looked contemptuously at me. He was now holding the Princess' limp form. "Shut up!" he taunted, "or you'll have the whole Hua-Tagor tribe upon us."

With that he turned and started into the forest, in the direction opposite that of the Hua-Tagor village.

I gathered myself up and to my feet. The pain was still pounding around me like the swarming of buzzing bees singing discordantly in my ears. But I managed to stagger forward. Then through the blaze of agony I charged upon the other man, a low animal noise uttering from my lips. Never had I felt such hatred for another human being.

Tekop heard the cry and immediately released Illa, all but dropping her onto the ground. He turned to face me. His body coiled, legs bent, braced for my charge. A dazed, surprised expression blanched his features.

I rammed into him with all the weight of my body. We slammed into the ground, tangled, rolled.

It was some time before I moved. Then I searched around. My hands found his thin pale neck. With the weight of my body pinning him down and my hands squeezing the scraggly throat, Tekop was completely helpless. His face turned dark, his lips contracted, his eyes seemed to bulge from their sockets. A large, puffy tongue snapped out between the gasping lips that could find no air.

I squeezed with every ounce of my strength in me. Then his face purpled and I felt his body go rigid, then shudder and lie still. I collapsed upon him, exhausted.

It was some time before I moved. When I stood, looked down at the dead form of Tekop. I felt no regret. He had deserved to die for his treachery.

Then I turned to Illa, who was sitting up, a blank expression on her face.

"Are you all right?" I inquired, standing over her, reaching down for her hands.

She shook her head. "I thought...he killed you."

"Not quite."

I pulled her up. Once she was standing, I said: "We better hurry. It is getting late. The Hua-Tagor might at any moment discover we are missing from the hut. This way."

We started for the beach, going in the direction Te-kop had said the small boats were possibly located. My ears were constantly alert for any sounds which might indicate that the savage Tagorians had discovered our disappearance and were pursuing us. Of course by this time we were quite far from their inland village, but if there was any sound of men going through the forest, I was determined to do my best to avoid discovery.

The beach narrowed up ahead, and then turned, disappearing to the right. Once we had rounded this point, we came to a large shoreline on which were some twenty long narrow rowboats. But also a couple of Tagorian warriors sat there on the beach, working.

They had not seen us, so I pulled Illa toward the forest. We went into the foliage which grew thick here, and slowly worked our way toward the two warriors who were laboring on one of the boats, patching its side.

When we were opposite them, I searched the immediate area for some heavy stick that might be used as a weapon. But there wasn't anything which I might use. For a moment I waited, unsure of the best plan of action. While I mentally floundered for some means of attacking the two men, a shout sounded down beach from where we had just come.

I turned to see several armed warriors emerge from around the curve of the beach and start toward the boats.

There was no time to hesitate. Either I managed to immediately overpower the two men, and get one of the boats into the water before the others arrived, or we were finished.

"Illa—*to the boats!*" Without looking to see if she followed directions, I rushed out into the open, leaping toward the two men who stood facing the approaching warriors.

CHAPTER FIVE

FLIGHT TO JORJOS

As I rushed toward the two Tagorian warriors, I could not help feeling that there wasn't a chance in a million of success. Yet the distance was gobbled up much faster than one might have imagined. I was upon the two men before they realized what had happened.

Shouts from those approaching up beach, attempting to warn their fellows of danger, seemed to confuse rather than help the pair.

I leaped at them, both arms spread wide on either side of me.

They were standing quite close together, and just as I gained striking distance one of them turned.

I slammed both arms together, gathering up each man's head. Every muscle was in use. The two heads connected with a mighty crush.

Without even waiting for them to fall to the ground, I turned, saw Illa struggling with one of the long boats, and rushed to her side.

The others were already running toward us, spears raised. They shouted for us to stop.

Swooping down, I lifted the light bark-covered long boat into my arms.

"Come!" I shouted, running toward the surf.

A moment later we were treading the icy water. I lowered the boat and shoved it forward.

"Quick—get in!" The boat was already beginning to float lazily on the surf.

A spear cut into the water and sand a few heads from me. I grabbed it as Illa climbed into the boat. The Tagorian warriors were within a spear cast.

I tossed the spear into the boat and pushed farther out into the water. A wave buckled lightly under us. I shoved farther out and then a moment later a larger wave almost overturned us. Illa had picked up an oar and was now attempting to help guide and balance the boat. Once we were beyond the breakers I attempted to crawl on board. At first it was impossible since the waves were momentarily too high. I waited until the wave had passed us and the boat had dropped to waist level. Then I pulled myself in behind Illa just in time to beat another swelling wave which carried us high upon its crest.

No sooner had I gotten into the boat than Illa screamed.

I turned to see a warrior come at us in the water. His spear was already thrusting out at me.

I ducked then grabbed the shaft of the spear and yanked it out of the startled man's hands. I swung the weapon around, hitting the Tagorian warrior on the side of the head. Another warrior was already beginning to get close. I reversed the spear and cast it at him. Its point went straight for his chest, sinking deep as red blood spurted. The man clutched at the shaft, then sank face forward into the water.

I turned, saw Illa rowing with one of the oars. Grabbing the other, I dipped it into the water on the opposite side.

The progress was slow at first for we had to fight the current of the waves which wanted to pull us back to shore. But I had pushed the craft beyond the real breakers, so finally our progress began to develop a slow steady speed that took us away from the Isle of Tagor.

Illa, who was looking back over her shoulder every once in a while, cried in alarm, "They are following."

I turned to see three boats enter the surf, manned with two warriors each.

"Stroke once on the left side, then on the right. Left, then right," I instructed the Princess, immediately taking a reverse rhythm; for in this was it would not be necessary to hold down my own stroke.

Every once on a while I looked behind us. The Princess was quickly getting tired. The other boats were already beginning to close the gap.

Luckily the waters were calm all the way to the horizon, and the sky clear blue. Off in the distance I could just make out the suggestion of land on the horizon. The sun was already beginning to blaze hotly down upon the calm, shimmering world of water. The island behind us was like some beautiful green jewel rising out of the clear blue ocean, coming to a sharp mountain-topped peak, almost like the point of a spear. It looked like a haven for lost seamen, where one would find beautiful princesses willing to share their lives forever with any weary traveler who might come their way— but it was quite the opposite: a hellish nightmare rock where the flesh of man was served as the only fit meat for warriors.

The other boats were coming closer. They were almost within spear casting distance.

Now I stroked with all the muscles in my arms and body, speeding the rhythm, but even so our progress was not fast enough. When I looked back I saw the nearest boat was much too close. One of the men was standing with spear raised back over his head.

"Down!" I grabbed hold of Illa's shoulder and shoved her face down into the bottom of the boat.

The man's arm flew forward. I swung my oar, holding it with both arms. The small wooden shaft splintered into the spear as the weapon shot through the air toward my chest. The spear sank into the water.

I quickly bent over the side of the boat and reached with the now broken oar, dragged the floating spear close, pulled it up. I stood carefully.

Balancing the spear in my hand, I drew my right arm back, then forward, almost overturning the boat as I released the weapon.

The point hit lower than I had hoped, and at first seemed to have missed its intended mark, sinking into the water just in front of the approaching boat. Then I heard a curse from one of the men.

I grinned, pleased, and without waiting took the oar from Illa and started rowing. I looked over my shoulder just long enough to see the other boat slowly sink into the ocean. My aim had been low, but not too low to miss its mark. And, as I had hoped, the other two crafts stopped to pick up their fellow warriors.

We had obtained a greater lead and after some time the boats of the Tagorians stopped and turned around, returning home. By then we were so far away from the island that it appeared to be but a small rock sticking out of the ocean.

Once I saw the others stop their pursuit I put down the oar and faced Illa, who had been sitting silently in the front of the boat.

"Are you all right, Princess?" I asked, gently, though it was easy to see that no harm had befallen her.

She nodded weakly. Her face was white, her cheeks sunk in deep with strained exhaustion.

Suddenly I realized that neither of us had taken a good sleep for a long time.

"Why don't you get some rest? I'll keep watch. It will be a while before we reach shore."

She nodded but said nothing. A moment later she was curled up in the bottom of the boat.

I looked out at the ocean surrounding us, toward the East, our destination: the shores of Jorjos. This was our second day since the storm. We were no closer to home than before—but the improvement from swimming to boating was much for which to be thankful.

For a moment I considered the possibility of turning course and attempting to row to Haldolen. Then I rejected the idea as quite impossible. It was at least several days' journey and without food and water we would never make it. There was always the chance of completely passing it in the night. Jorjos, on the other hand, was within sight. Dangers surely lay there, but also we had a far better chance of survival—and reaching the lands beyond, which were friendly to Haldolen and God-Lord Muda. As perilous as that course might seem, it would be far less dangerous than attempting to cross the Haldolen Ocean without food or water; and even with such food there was the chance of another storm, which would surely bring death.

The sun burned its way up into the heavens. The rocking of the boat, as it slowly drifted toward the land off in the distance, gradually hypnotized me into a half sleep. There was no awareness of actually drifting off course but all of a sudden I heard movement. My eyes jerked open and saw Illa was just sitting up at the other end of the boat. She turned, smiled.

The day was already darkening, the sun casting red fires across the world to paint Illa's face with highlights of orange. She looked at me, then laughed.

"You should see yourself, Thoris of Rota."

"What's wrong?"

"Your face is filthy! After all that digging, no wonder." She grew serious for a moment, then looked abruptly sad. "I wonder what made Tekop turn on us as he did."

"Probably had the same plan for you that the Hua-Tagors had." Or worse, I thought with a shudder. Then I dipped my hands into the salt water. A few moments later my face felt cleaner.

Then I turned my attention to the East for the first time since awakening and realized that we had made amazing progress during our sleep.

A line of mountains stretched from North to South almost as far as one could see, rising high into the skies. At their base was a thickness of dark green, where jungles grew thick; below that a thin line of whitish yellow indicated a beach. But all this was still a long distance off. It would be quite dark by the time we reached the shore. After our last experience on land at night, I hesitated to fall into the same kind of trap.

Illa noticed the direction of my gaze and turned. "Oh look! How beautiful!"

"Beautiful, yes. But I wish we were closer. I want to have time to land before dark and find a good place in which to keep undercover." I picked up the oar as I spoke, and started moving it in and out of the water, taking up a rhythm that swung it from the left side of the boat to the right.

Overhead was the sound of birds chirping. Several white gulls swooped down to investigate us, then flew away toward the East, and land.

As we drew closer and closer to shore, the red fires of Fahda the Sun dipped lower into the ocean, as if in some perverted race with us. But this was the kind of race we could not possibly win. Slowly the Sun sank under the horizon, first its bottom half, then finally the top, which dwindled away until only the suggestion of light flared in the West. Black night was already painted in the East and the first twinkling of stars taunted us as we crept toward the distant shore. Then even the twilight disappeared and total night fluttered into being.

Silence echoed all around us; there was only the soft splash of my oar, as it dipped into the waters, to relieve the quiet. Neither of us spoke. My ears strained to hear the sound of surf but the stillness remained to taunt and tease like the touch of an evil spirit.

Yet there was a strange peacefulness to the night, as if we were the only two in the world. I could almost imagine us as two normal mortals, man and woman, in a savage primitive land where there were no rules nor social regulations, no levels of social order; and where royal princesses would not exist for another thousand years or more—and man could take the woman he most desired with nobody to argue the point. But this was not a primitive world. Civilization had touched man, and given us Gods to worship and a Living-God to rule over us, and Royalty to obey and serve. Levels of status. And I, warrior, a Commoner by birth, could never even wish for the hand of Princess Illa except in my most quiet inner thoughts. We were civilized. Illa a princess. I a servant. So only at moments like these, when even Gods were sleeping and could not listen to my innermost thoughts, was I allowed to dream that Illa was a mere woman and I her equal.

Then Lonu the Moon rose and brought soft pale light upon the world.

Distantly came a soft murmuring which slowly grew louder.

Illa turned, looked into the dimness beyond our boat.

"We are close," she murmured.

The dream mood passed and reality stiffened my muscles, moved them into quicker action. The oar cut into the waters from left to right, back and forth across the narrow boat, steering it toward the shores of Jorjos.

The sound of breakers hitting the beach grew louder and the lifting of the ocean under us gained a new, more powerful rhythm. In the pale moonlight I finally managed to see the shore, the dim pasty sand and dark looming jungle beyond.

We were picked up and shot forward on the crest of a wave which subsided a few seconds later. We held onto the sides of the frail boat. The sound of breakers was now much louder. Another wave picked up the craft. We moved ahead, then fell behind, sucked back to meet another wave. This time the crest carried us almost to its breaking point.

I grabbed the spear, in case we were tossed overboard on the next wave.

The boat rocked up and down, dipped violently. Abruptly another wave struck us. For a moment I believed the boat would overturn, than all at once we shot forward like an arrow, straight for the beach. Illa laughed in pleasure and I felt a slight flicker of relief as we were shoved up onto the sand.

The water receded, but even before it had slipped back into the mother ocean I was out of the boat, reaching for Illa.

"Come," I said, "follow me."

The spear was held in my hands, ready for an emergency, as we stepped forward, leaving the sandy beach behind.

Illa kept close to me. Her hand touched the harness strap which went over the right shoulder. Neither of us said a word as we moved into the dark thickness of the tangled vegetation.

Shortly I came to a stop in front of a tree which had fruit-like substances growing on its branches. I pulled on one of the branches, yanked from it what turned out to be an orange-colored round fruit. I gave it to Illa and started gathering more. Even though I was sick of the diet of fruit, anything seemed good at the moment. I could hardly wait to feast on our find.

We each took an armful of the fruit and then back-tracked our way to the beach. There we made a small camp near the trunk of a large gnarled tree.

After finishing off our supply of fruit, I stood, started moving along the edge of the jungle growth to gather wood, then stopped short, thinking better of it. The last time we had done that it had led to capture by the Tagorians.

Haldolen had no knowledge of what kind of inhabitants lived on Jorjos, other than that they were called Ijans and had refused all form of trade or communication. They were supposed to be civilized but nobody had investigated for several generations so I was not about to take any unnecessary chances. They might be savages much like the Tagorians—or worse. Our explorers had made it a habit of going around Jorjos because there were seemingly endless lands to explore—more than we needed at this time.

I returned to Illa, sat down.

"What'd you do?" she asked.

"I was going to get wood for a fire."

"I'm cold. Why aren't you getting the wood?" She rubbed her arms.

"We don't want to take any chances. It's best we remain here, without a fire, and make the best of it. Discovery by the Ijans would mean immediate capture."

"Yes...you are right." She leaned back against the trunk of the tree and closed her eyes. "The night is warm enough, anyway."

I watched her for a moment, fascinated by the rising and falling of her breast under the *tuda*. How lovely and desirable she looked.

Her eyes suddenly opened. "What are you staring at?"

"You, Princess."

"Well don't! It makes me nervous!" She hesitated, took a deep labored breath that expanded her lungs, then asked: "Why?"

"You are beautiful to look at," I said huskily.

"You have no right to speak that way to me. You should know better!" she scolded, but her voice was far from angry.

"What is wrong with telling your Princess that she is beautiful—when she surely is very beautiful?" Sudden passion made me foolishly bold.

"It is just wrong, that's all!" She pouted, then closed her eyes. "Go to sleep!"

I turned and looked out to the ocean. The waves broke on the shore like a shattering string of diamonds, rushing up the sands in foamy brightness only to reluctantly recede and disappear into a new string of diamonds. The boat which had brought us safely to land floated a short distance out in the water. For a moment I considered going after it, brining it to the beach, then changed my mind. There was no place we could go in it.

"Why do you think I'm beautiful?" Princess Illa murmured from behind me.

I turned. She was staring at me in a very curious way. Her eyes glowed. The long hair flowed over her shoulders in lengthy curled waves, reflecting a soft glow from the moonlight.

"Just that you are very beautiful!" I shot back, irritated and not knowing why. "Now, go to sleep!"

"Don't tell me what to do!" Her eyes blazed, fiery.

"Please, Princess. You will need rest. Tomorrow I will hunt for some meat. I'll make a bow and some arrows," I told her. "And then we will start the long march through these lands, and attempt to reach Andus, where Dahsa is Ruler in the name of your father. It will be a long and hard journey and I want to make it as quickly as possible. So...you will need your rest."

She was silent for a moment, then after a while she asked: "Why don't you pay me the respect due a Princess?"

"I do."

"But you order me around as I were *your* subject. I am not a slave! I could have you whipped for the way you have ordered me around as if I were your slave." She made a face but there was something about her which was so appealing that my heart went out to tenderly embrace her. But I was resolved to make her realize the truth of our situation.

"In the land of Jorjos it might be better for you if you *were* my slave. I think it best that both of us strip our clothing of all rank and national identity. It is best for us to be regarded as simple wanderers here in Jorjos. I, as a warrior for hire, you my slave," I explained as gently as possible. Then a little more angrily, being piqued by her air of superiority, I added, "And, anyway, I only lead to bring you to safety. Once you are safely in the hands of friends, you may punish me as you think proper for any offense for which I might be responsible. In the meantime, please, Princess, realize that I am only doing my duty. I am sworn to protect your life and I am willing to do so with my own, if necessary."

"Because I am your princess?" she inquired in an oddly strained voice?

"Because you are my Princess and—" I started to add, *because I love you,* but just in time stopped myself.

"And what?" Illa demanded.

"And..."

"Well?"

"Because you are the daughter of our God-Lord Muda!" I finished lamely.

Turning away from her, I lay on my back, looked up at the starry night which twinkled down at me. I heard Illa start to say something, then silence followed.

I lay there for some time thinking about what lay ahead of us and inwardly shuddering at the dangers which would no doubt stand in our way to safety. Capture would mean instant death for Illa, if the Ijans ever realized who she was. I would have given almost anything for a good long sword and a unit of Haldolen warriors to escort the princess to our destination.

It was some time before sleep claimed all worries, all fears, and gave me a much needed rest.

CHAPTER SIX

OPIL OF ZORKADA

The sun was bright and hot when I once again opened my eyes. Off in the distance was the soft sound of feminine humming.

I turned to see Illa wading in the foamy ocean. The hot tropic sun was already one-fourth into the sky. There was no sign of the boat which had brought us to land.

I sat watching Princess Illa play in the water like a little girl, splashing all around as the waves rolled in and out. She suddenly dipped down and worked water over her bare arms. She turned, saw me, and called a cheery hello.

"Why don't you come in? It feels fine!" she cried happily.

"I should think you'd have had enough of water in the last couple of days." A sense of inner warmth and pleasure surged through me. It seemed as if we were both in some strange mystical paradise. How wonderful it would be to have lived thus for the rest of our lives. "How can you stand it?"

"Oh, this is different!" Her head twisted around, swinging the long blond hair in the air around her shoulders. "In the morning it is wonderful!"

I thought about the change which was already evident in Illa. The last comments of the night before now teased my brain—for Princess Illa had then seemed more ordinary woman than one of royal birth, with her coy feminine questions. And now she also seemed less like royalty and more like any other female of Haldolen at happy play in the morn-

65

ing surf. The fact that Illa had stripped from her gown all minute details which might indicate royalty helped in this illusion. Now, instead of golden clips and braided belt, she wore from all outward appearances a common tuda of white, having also removed her outer, more colorful clothes.

No one would have guessed that in the last few days we had gone through what must have seemed a most horrifying series of experiences for the princess—a woman who had been coddled and pampered all her life in the Temple of Lord-Muda, her father, Ruler of all Haldolen, the Living-God of our people.

I turned my attention to the crude Tagorian spear which had come with me from the isle of Tagor. It was a starkly primitive weapon, made of forest wood, roughly splintered, with a sharpened flint stone for its point, lashed tightly into place with animal hide. But there was a good balance to the shaft. It made a remarkably usable weapon; and it was the only one I now had, since the Tagorians had stripped me of knife and short sword. With this spear I could easily bring down an animal, which would serve as our first real meal since we left the galley *Vayis*. My body hungered for meat. We would need great strength for the long journey before us. We must cross the lands of Jorjos and find the colony of Andus where Dahsa ruled in the name of Muda and where Princess Illa would be safe.

I called to the Princess, saying that I would be right back. Then I stood, taking the spear in my right hand,

"Where are you going, Thoris?" She turned to look at me.

"Hunting."

"I'll come with you." She ran up the short beach, the shorter and looser fitting tuda flowing gently around her curvy legs.

"It might be better if you stayed here," I carefully suggested.

"No. I don't want to be separated again. And that's final!" Illa stared up into my face, her deep green eyes stubbornly set.

She seemed so defenseless. And I would gladly have died for her. I loved her, but hopelessly so. She was my princess. Yet how desirable. And how mighty and proud her regal manner; commanding; demanding. Still she had been willing to do her share when it had been necessary.

"Alright, come. But be quiet. We will have to move like shadows in the jungle. For animals have ears that hear from far way. They smell with the speed of the wind. We must keep up—"

"On occasion I have hunted with my father's warriors," Illa interrupted. "So I know the manner in which we will catch our morning meal!"

She motioned me in front of her.

"Keep close, Princess."

"I intend to," she assured me in a strangely tense and sincere voice.

We entered the outer fringes of the jungle and soon were swallowed up by the vegetation which grew rapidly thick. We were forced to change our course many times as we moved around the thickets and thorn bushes that spanned great distances on all sides. Before long I had lost track of which direction we were going. The sound of the beach had totally disappeared, now to be replaced by the jungle songs of birds and chatter of smaller and larger creatures. I could not have returned to the beach if I'd wanted to. I thanked the Gods that Illa had insisted on coming along for otherwise I would never have seen her again.

The vegetation which surrounded us was strikingly beautiful. Even in our thickest forest in central Haldolen we have nothing like what I found surrounding us now. Varied colors popped out at us at every turn, designed in the pattern of lovely, delicately formed flowers which looked as if they would shatter into dust if touched. Birds of long hard beaks, of flashing plumage, of trilling voices, were like a choir of the Temple virgins. And beyond this, carrying on an alien conversation between themselves, were the chattering, leaping monkeys who swung through the trees' upper foliage.

The birds and even the monkeys looked like desperation food, so I let my spear ignore them, searching for heavier, juicer game.

Fahda the Sun burned down like the flames of fire; the insistent humming of insects played harshly on the morning air.

We passed several fruit trees and reluctantly picked our morning breakfast and drink. This type of diet was wearing thin on my stomach.

We had traveled for some time. The day passed from early morning to early midday without any sign of the kind of game I so desperately sought. I was about to give up all hope and fell a likely bird or monkey, when we suddenly came upon a meadow which spread for some distance from left to right, covered by thick, ankle high grass.

Then I saw a herd of deer off to our right. Suddenly they jerked to attention, their heads flashed upright, ears rose high, eyes turned. Then all at once they leaped into motion, heading madly in our direction.

At first I thought what great luck we were having but they passed so swiftly that it was quite impossible to even ready myself to cast the spear at one of them.

"What could have caused that?" Illa wondered.

I motioned her to silence as the herd disappeared. When the noise of their stampede faded, the distinct sound of metal clashing against metal came to our ears.

"Fighting! A battle," I said with sudden surprise.

My first impulse was to go the other direction—a far safer course of action. Then a scream sounded, and there was no doubt that it was that of a woman in holy terror of her life. I reconsidered my first impulse. It sounded like a small battle, and not far from us. There seemed to be no more than four or five warriors involved. And a woman.

Immediately I decided to carefully investigate. And in any case, there was at least a chance to get weapons from dead warriors who might be left behind.

I motioned Illa to follow me as I made my way toward the ring of metal on metal.

We crossed the clearing and continued for about a thousand heads before coming to a bend in the meadow, where it turned off to our right. Beyond that came the sound of combat.

I pulled Illa into the brush. "Stay here!"

Without looking back, I crept forward, hidden behind a screen of foliage as I rounded the bend and came within sight of a small skirmish.

Immediately I took the scene in and made an impulsive, snap decision.

There were three yellow-garbed warriors fighting against a lonesome swordsman who protected a small dark-haired woman in blue who always kept behind her lone defender. There were several dead men laying on the ground; five of these were obviously members of the attacking force. Apparently the woman and two men had been ambushed by eight men in yellow.

The lone warrior was already cut to pieces, blood spattered over his blue clothing, and would not last long. His harness and uniform were sliced in half a dozen places. His sword arm was already failing him. Shortly he would be run through if something was not done, and fast. What was then destined for his woman, I could only guess—and those guesses weren't pretty.

I hesitated, unsure how wise it might be to get involved. I knew nothing as to who was in the right—who might offer friendship. Yet, the fact remained that one side was unfairly outnumbered. This man in blue continued in vain to protect the helpless woman, knowing that he would die in the attempt. This blind bravery, more than anything else, moved me to identify with him. This man could easily be myself defending the Princess.

My first impulse was to use the spear as a club-like weapon but instead I hesitated long enough to cast it at the yellow warrior about to cut down the woman's protector from the side.

The spear flew through the air straight on target, striking the warrior in the back, driving through to come out the other side, blood red.

At the same time I was swooping down to where one of the dead men lay. Grabbing hold of the long sword I yelled loudly to attract attention.

The feel of the slender sword in my hand was like gaining some strange eerie power. The force surged through

69

every muscle. A grim smile formed on my lips as I leaped forward.

One of the two enemy warriors turned. His sword lashed out in a wicked thrust which I easily parried with the tip of my long bladed sword.

The man in blue, whom I had come to succor, seemed to gain a new spurt of energy. But his strength had drained both from exhaustion and loss of blood. He had no chance of survival. His sword arm would soon fail him.

I engaged my man with intent to kill, immediately and without mercy. My sword flashed from left to right, lunged, sliced, cut, creating a net of razor-sharp death before me. The warrior I faced was no match for my sword yet he managed to keep the point of my weapon away from his body for a few moments by stepping back, parrying, and side-stepping the first series of attacks. But on the third feint and lunge, my sword found an easy opening, slipping swiftly in, then out of the other's chest.

The man's sword fell to the ground and his knees buckled under him. A moment later he was face down in the grass, dead.

The warrior in blue took a cut to the left side, another across the stomach, a third in the thigh, as I headed toward the two combatants.

"Here!" My sword engaged the enemy's weapon before he actually realized what had happened, as the point was flung up into the air.

Then my sword lashed out, found the center of the man's chest and pressed deep, running through to the hilt. I let the sword fall with the dead body and turned to face the wounded warrior and the raven-haired woman.

The man in the strange blue clothing, which hugged tightly across his body from feet to neck—much the same as the yellow-garbed men—was lying on the ground, staring weakly up at me.

"Who are...you?" he whispered between blood covered lips.

"A friend," I offered carefully, looking to the woman, who was standing close by, a frightened, drawn expression on her pretty, pert little face.

70

"Friend," said the dying warrior as he turned to gaze at the woman. "Take Opil back to her father...you will be highly rewarded..." his lips hung wide apart for a moment, his eyes closed, then fluttered open. He looked blankly at me, then fell backwards to the ground without another word.

I turned to the woman whom the man had called Opil.

She was holding a hand over her lips. For a moment she stood there unmoving, then suddenly recovered with amazing speed. "He was truly a brave warrior. I will have my father raise a great feast every fourth-season in his honor!"

"What do we do with these men?" I made a sweep of the dead but ended with the warrior who had died so bravely in her defense.

"We will have our men pick *those* up," she indicated the yellow uniformed men, "and feed them to the dogs." Then with softened voice she finished: "As for Dosa and Gelt, we will burn their bodies in the Great Tower with all honors."

"You will leave them here now?"

"What else can we do?" Her voice was puzzled. "We must first go to my father's castle."

"Where is it?"

"Not far from here. Great Xalla will reward you, mighty warrior. I owe my life to you and I will never forget this!" She stepped forward, he lips wide with a warm, inviting smile. Her dark, haunting eyes gazed up into mine and for a moment I had the strangest feeling that I had known her forever—that I could look into her very spirit and read the thoughts, the dreams, the emotions there. "What can Opil, daughter of the Wizard of Zorkada, call you, mighty warrior?"

"Thoris..."

"Thoris...what?"

"Just Thoris, a warrior—and adventurer!" I quickly added, believing that this might satisfy her, and thankful for having no sign of Haldolen armies on my harness.

"Thoris the Mighty!" Opil exclaimed in her low, husky voice. She was a slender, sunken-cheeked woman, with a well filled-out body. She was a little shorter than Illa and quite the opposite in every outward, physical way. Her hair was short, her lips full, almost too well-padded, her eyes dark and mysteriously veiled. It was hard to fathom the depth or honesty of her warmth. "Thoris the Mighty, I am eternally in your debt."

She reached a small slender hand out for mine, and it took it in hers, squeezing gently. "Opil of Zorkada is your friend for life."

Then she stepped back. "From whence do you come?"

"Far away. I have no country."

At that point Illa came out of the foliage of the jungle and stepped toward us.

"Who is *that?*" Opil demanded, her eyes immediately flashing.

"This is Illa...my...*slave!*" I threw a warning glance at Illa, and silently prayed to all the Gods of Rota and Haldolen, real or dreamed of, that she would play along with my claim. Her life might depend on it, for if the people of Jorjos were to discover she was the Princess of Haldolen, they might automatically kill her.

Amazingly, Illa bowed. "Illa, slave of...Thoris the *Mighty!*" There was just a hint of sarcasm in her voice but I don't believe Opil noticed.

"She is a pretty slave!" Opil observed as she glanced up at me. There was an odd mocking expression in her eyes. "She is just a slave?"

"Nobody is *just* a slave!" I countered, worried. Over Opil's shoulders Illa made an angry face at me. But the expression in her eyes was just as puzzling as the look in Opil's.

I was frantically praying that I would handle the situation properly. Opil, whose father sounded ominous, could prove to be a boon—or an extreme danger. I even thought of killing her, in order to save Princess Illa from any personal harm but swiftly rejected the idea as unintelligent and unnecessarily brutal. I had saved Opil's life and she rightly believed that this put her in my debt. Yet, something in the look of her eyes, the turn of her lips in that warm smile, set a warning bell wildly ringing in my head.

Then she took hold of my right hand, gripped it firmly in hers, and started to draw me off across the meadow.

"Wait!" I pulled my hand free, then went over to one of the dead warriors. After stripping the man of waist harness, which supported sword and knife sheaths, I buckled it over the one around my waist, then picked up one of the fallen swords and slipped it into the sheath at my right. "It's better to be armed."

I glanced meaningfully at Illa.

"This slave of yours wears beautiful clothes—if not a little torn and dirty," Opil accused. "Her hair is too bland, her body too tall. She is too thin to be pretty."

Opil was standing almost within arms reach of Illa, with hands on hips. The expression that twisted her face was harsh, cutting. The tone of her voice was like ice. *"She is not strong!"*

"She is faithful!" I quickly offered, seeing the start of anger flash to Illa's face.

"A dog is faithful!" Opil spat out. She possessively took my arm and started out across the meadow.

I glanced over my shoulder at Illa, who was now stony-faced, lips compressed, eyes hot with controlled anger. But she remained silent. She knew I was attempting to save her life—not humiliate her.

"Why were you attacked?" I inquired, turning my attention to Opil.

"The Vistars are always at war with the Zorkada. They attacked, hoping to take me captive. No doubt to stop my father from using his powers. The war has continued for a long time. They want the lands of the East here, and our great Ruler is not about to give them away. It is an old war, battling over the borders of our lands. One would think people could learn to get along with one another—instead of fighting and killing all the time. My father's magic has helped the Ruler of Zorkada—and has kept our smaller nation victorious for 50 seasons."

She frowned, looked up at me. Her lips compressed, prettily. "And what about you? What are you doing in our lands?"

"We were washed ashore during the storm two days ago. Since then we have wandered the lands of...Jorjos—I must admit I'm quite lost." I was aware of the warmth of her fingers in mine. She was being a little too friendly.

"You were lucky not to have been captured by the Vistars before now. They would have put you to death in their Arena. But then, so would the Zorkadas—though not now, for you have saved my life, and both my father, Xalla and Hillis, our High Ruler, will be grateful. And so will I, for the rest of my days!"

Out of the corner of my eye I could see Illa just barely half a step behind. I turned, looked at her, asked: "How are you, Illa?" the question was not important, but just noticing and recognizing her seemed the right thing to do.

She did not answer at first. Then after a long pause, she said: "Fine."

Opil cursed. "It is the same all over the world, I see! Slaves are slaves! You should beat her."

"I do not believe in beating a slave," I quickly announced before Opil got any ideas of suggesting I do so or Illa became convinced I might have to.

"You do not beat your slave? What keeps her in her place?" Opil's voice was thick with amazement.

"Respect. She knows I will take care of her, and feed her, and protect her life—and she fulfills her duties for me in return." I was half afraid it might sound too farfetched.

"She seems more like your *woman* than your slave." Opil accused. There was a mixture of hatred, anger in her dark eyes.

"A slave is a far better servant when treated fairly!" I stated with the ring of authority in my voice.

Illa put in: "My master is a great warrior. I am *honored* to be his slave."

It was almost convincing even to me.

"Where did you get this...*slave?"* It was obvious that Opil did not like Illa.

"I saved her life from a cruel master whom I had to kill. She has been with me ever since." I was suddenly enjoying myself.

I studied Opil more carefully. She was wearing a dark blue gown which hung in wavy folds over her shoulders, completely covering them, then falling to the ground to her feet. The gown was strapped in the middle with a braided gold waistband. She was a beautiful woman—though something in those dark eyes was violent.

We continued in silence for some time, then Opil suddenly led us to the left, into a narrow jungle path.

"Along this path is the magnificent castle of my father, the Wizard of Zorkada. I was on my morning stroll with my two personal bodyguards when we were attacked. The third man was a friend. He was a proud warrior who had placed his heart before me. But...men will do that. I am sorry for him." Dropping my arm she stepped in front of me.

"Follow close, and don't allow those long creeping vines to touch you!" She pointed to dark green vines which grew along the path in great numbers. "They will grab and strangle the life from you bodies. Don't be fooled by the thinness of the vines! They are powerful enough to snare and trap a mountain lion."

"How?" Illa gasped. "How can this be?"

Opil jerked around, glared at Illa with the open hatred of a tigress for another female cat. "A slave in my country is seen and not heard!"

"How?" I quickly inquired before any further exchange could pass between the two women.

"My father is a wizard!" she announced with great pride, as if that fully explained the matter. Then, as we came to a sudden turn in the pathway, she stopped, stepped aside, pointed: "And there is the castle of Xalla!"

I stepped forward. Behind me, Illa gasped as she looked upon the strange and eerie scene before us.

I had never conjured up in my wildest dreams such an odd structure. It was a huge, gleaming building which rose some twenty men into the sky. It was not constructed of blocks of stone, as the buildings of Haldolen, but of some strange blue-gray substance which was shiny like glass and seemed to be in one solid piece. The shape of the building was simplicity itself, being that of a huge tall oval-topped blocked with smooth rounded corners. A small river moat ran around the building and there was a large bridge, hung at a 45 degree angle in the air on chains. Many small windows lined the structure halfway up and were large enough for a man to stand in. Low grass grew around the moat, extending to the very edge of the clearing in which the castle was built. The circumference of the building was as large as the pyramid of Muda.

"Come, you will be welcome here!" Opil announced. Then she stepped forward into the clearing, motioning us to follow.

The moment we appeared in full sight of the huge castle of Xalla the Wizard, a loud trumpet blared from deep inside the building and the huge drawbridge fell into place with a loud clatter. Hardly had it come to rest than a dozen horsemen, clad in the bright color of yellow, came charging out towards us.

Before I could do a thing in our defense, they had surrounded us, drawn swords in hands. Two dismounted and approached me, swords threatening.

Opil cringed close to me and gave out a low scream of alarm and terror. She slipped to the ground, unconscious.

What I had immediately guessed to be true on seeing the colors of those tight fitting, full bodied uniforms on the horsemen, was now substantiated.

The two men stopped in front of me. Their swords were only a head from my stomach.

"Your weapon!" the tallest warrior demanded. "You are a prisoner of the Vistars. You will surrender or die!"

CHAPTER SEVEN

THE CASTLE OF XALLA

I reluctantly surrendered my sword to the Vistar warriors for there was nothing else for me to do other than die uselessly—which would do little to help my Princess.

We were immediately escorted through the grassy meadow and across the drawbridge, which was made of the same material as the walls of the castle of Xalla—though pebbly with a rough surface upon which it was possible to walk or ride without slipping. The walls of the castle were smooth, as they had looked from a distance. We passed through the huge metal gate and into the courtyard beyond.

Illa had hung close to me from the beginning, her hands clutching my left arm. The unconscious Opil was carried by one of the Vistar warriors.

As soon as all the mounted warriors had left the bridge it quickly swung up, half closed, hanging in the air like the gaping mouth of some weird monster.

I found myself in a strange, large open area, surrounded by walls much like the outside, glassy smooth; but here there were many narrow tall doors and windows lining the face of the building; staircases ran up to each floor. A huge golden double door faced opposite the gate. A giant dragon-like snake was carved around these doors with bulging evil eyes peering out at us from a head that hung high over the top of the entrance. A forked tongue lashed out beyond the large pointed curved fangs. This serpent head was twice the size of a man's head and had been carved in such magnificent detail that one found it hard to believe that it was not actually alive.

"Come!" One of the guards shoved us toward the large double doors below the dragon-snake.

I was thinking that if this immense serpent were alive I would never want to be within reach of that ugly head. What chance would mortal man have against such a creature of Hell?

"What's going to happen to us?" Princess Illa hissed in my ear.

"Follow my lead!" I whispered back, a plan already beginning to form in my mind. Maybe there was a chance of appearing as friends rather than enemies. After all, the Zorkadians and the Vistarians were equally known to us—and no doubt each considered us enemies. If I could convince the Vistarian leader that I was a friend, it would be safer for Illa. After that I would be in a far better situation to possibly help Opil and her father, if it seemed a safe thing to do. I would not endanger Illa, no matter what!

The doors opened silently as we approached. I expected to find men behind it—and was surprised to find nobody in sight. A queasy chill shivered along my spine.

A long hall extended before us, upon whose walls were colorful paintings of warriors in red and yellow. At the end of the hall on the ceiling was a picture of a white-bearded man, arms extended so that they were painted on the side walls. He was robed in black and from his outstretched fingers shafts of light shot towards the battling warriors, some running through the bodies of yellow and red garbed men as they writhed in agony.

The door below this bearded man was night-black with specks of light flickering in it. As I approached it seemed as if the door were slightly transparent and that one could see twinkling stars embedded deep. It was an illusion; a very weird one.

These doors opened as we approached, and this time I was not quite as startled to discover nobody beyond to open them. Nevertheless an icy chill tingled over every nerve in my body.

Illa seemed unimpressed. But she had seen the Wizard of Muda many times in the past and no doubt found little here that was new. Still her form pressed slightly closer to me.

I found myself in a small, yet very high-ceilinged, throne room which was walled in black drapes. The throne was large, black, twinkling in three dimensions with bright golden specks. A glistening smoothness had been polished on the material's surface. The chair was tall-backed with plain squared arms. On the seat of the throne was a soft-looking black cushion upon which sat a rather tall bearded man, dressed in a bright yellow robe-like cape which closed over his hollow chest, clasped at top under a triple circle of glittering gold. The man's face was sallow, the skin pulled tight around sharp angular bones. The eyes were narrow slits that watched carefully as we were directed toward the raised disk upon which sat the throne. The man's mouth was hard, thin and cruel. There was no evidence of mercy on his face.

"These two, who are they?" The man pointed a gnarled finger at us as we were stopped in front of him.

One of the guards bowed low. "Lord Waja, we found them with Opil. They were approaching the castle. We do not know what happened to the men we sent out for her—possibly they are dead. These two and Opil were walking."

"Who are you?" Lord Waja demanded in a high-pitched squeak of a voice. His eyes never left us.

"I am Thoris, and this is my slave, Illa. We are wanderers, having no country and no immediate allegiance." I bowed low. "I do not know why your men have taken us prisoners."

The man's mouth grinned thinly, his eyes narrowed. After some time he asked: "What are you doing in Jorjos?"

"We were swept ashore during the storm some days since," I explained, keeping to the story I had told Opil. "We but desire passage through the country. We mean no harm to anyone."

"You are either lying or a fool!" The Vistar Lord nodded thoughtfully for a moment. "I, Lord Waja, say there are only enemies or friends of The Vistars. You are not friends—so you must be enemies."

"Why must we be enemies?"

"I do not know you. I have not heard of you. You are not a friend."

"I would *be* your friend!" I quickly fired back.

"Because you are in my power now?" He grinned oilily. "Or because you are for my cause?"

"Does it make much difference? My sword is for those who will buy it. I am willing to sell my sword and my allegiance."

"You have no sword to sell!" Waja laughed. "I see my men have taken your teeth. What do I need with a swordsman who can so easily be taken prisoner?" He seemed to be enjoying himself. It was a game, and he would be the winner.

"I was outnumbered," I commented conversationally. "I do not believe that you will find a better swordsman in your ranks, or all of Jorjos."

Waja glared at me, then his lips opened and a loud contemptuous laugh trembled past them. "You have a brash mouth!" he finally snarled, leaning forward in the throne. "I have a swordsman in my unit who is the greatest in all the world! He has defeated every man to come up against him. He has killed hundreds in private duels, from all the states of Jorjos. And you would suggest that you are better than this man—the greatest of all Champions?"

"He has only fought lesser swordsmen than himself. I have never met a man who could defeat me!" I felt Illa's fingers dig into my arm as if to silence me. But already I saw the direction of the man's reasoning. There was little hope for us in any case, for this Lord Waja could easily have both of us killed—or worse, have me killed and then take Princess Illa for himself. His eyes had several times turned to her trim figure, sparked with interest. So I realized there was nothing to lose.

"I do not think your man can defeat me! And I'm willing to prove it to you—and him."

Lord Waja considered my open challenge, his right hand rubbing the thick black pointed beard at the end of his narrow chin. "It would be sport to see him cut you to pieces, warrior. But..."

80

He shrugged, turned his attention to the guards who had brought us here. "Take them away. We don't have time for light matters, yet. I will consider your challenge. In the meantime you will be confined in the dungeons. Take them."

He waved his right arm toward Illa. "The woman. She is to be kept in the highest rooms of the tower, with the Wizard's daughter."

The man grinned, looked at me for a moment. "I don't think a slave needs a slave. Do you?"

"You refuse my offer of friendship?" I shot back hotly, much as a man might after making a really honest offer.

"I reject nothing—yet! We will see." The man waved and one of the guards grabbed hold of my right arm, shoved me toward the exit.

I was taken out of the room behind Illa. Then we were separated. The guard roughly directed me to the door on our right, which opened automatically at our approach. There was a staircase leading down into semi-darkness. At the bottom was a long hallway, lined on both sides with small metal doors with large slip bolts. The guard opened one of these doors, pushed me inside.

"How about food, water?" I requested as the man started to close the door.

He laughed. "A dead man needs no food!"

Then the door clanged shut, the bolt slipped into place. I was submerged in total darkness. There was no exit from the cell other than one bolted door.

I stood there for a long time, listening. I waited for my eyes to become used to the darkness. But the black kept pressing in without relief and finally I realized it was not going to get any lighter. Then it was that I blindly examined my cell with outstretched arms. It proved to be made of block stone that was damp to touch. It was not much larger than the length of a tall man's body. There was no bedding; only the floor to sleep on.

"Now what?" I addressed the darkness around me. But, of course, there was no answer. Not at first, at least.

I was just beginning to sit down when I heard a soft hissing voice which seemed to talk through the walls.

"Who are you?" the crackling voice softly whispered as if floating on the air itself.

"Who are *you?}*" I cried, alarmed. I immediately stood, gazed blankly into the inky night.

"Xalla. I felt your presence in the cell next to mine. Who are you, stranger?" The voice spoke more loudly this time. But now it seemed to come on the air around me rather than through the thickness of solid stone.

"Thoris of Rota. A friend, if you will have one."

"I cannot be particular. We are both captives in my own castle. Whom should I turn to? How did you happen to be captured?" The voice was old, crackling.

"We found your daughter being attacked by the Vistars and -"

"My daughter?" The voice almost screamed, as if in the cell with me. "Is she all right? Have they harmed her?"

"The last I saw of her she was well—alive and unharmed."

"Where did you last see her?"

"As we were brought in here." I then related in detail what had happened since first hearing the sound of battle in the jungle until the present time, leaving out only such details as would have revealed Illa as anything other than my slave.

"This slave of yours," the voice said when I was finished, "is in great danger."

"Aren't all of us?"

There was silence, then: "Come, let me have a look at you."

I started to say something but the words froze like icicles in my throat. Every muscle curled tight in reaction to what I suddenly saw. I drew back, pressed against the wall.

Opposite me was a dimly glowing light which forced its way *through* the stone. The glow was working inside the stone as if it were transparent glass. Then slowly the glowing light swelled in size, took shape. And abruptly it was in the cell with me.

At first I was looking at a misty human-like form, then slowly the mist cleared while the light remained. There, standing before me, was a small, shriveled man with a long

82

white beard which came to a ragged point just below his lower ribs. His robe was gray, marked with strange symbols of gold. The man's face was a map of wrinkles, the eyes sparkling fires of deep blue.

"I am Xalla, Wizard of Zorkada!" the apparition announced with a low bow which made his robes rustle. "I like what I see!" he exclaimed after a moment of silent contemplation. His face had shriveled up like a dried fruktar as he studied me; it was a mad complex of wrinkled smiles. "You look like a true friend. A man of honor."

"How—how did you come in here?" I gasped, unable to believe what my eyes saw, even though I was aware that Wizards were supposed to have strange and magical powers.

"I am not really here, but my eyes are looking at you, and the form you see is an illusion of myself which I have impressed on your mind. But, enough of that! I would not give you the secrets of Wizardry! Come, come, you say you have saved my daughter's life. For that you will be rewarded. Though I am surely not in any position to do so now. I am sorry for the loss of my two men—but you, apparently, have been sent to save us from those evil men of Vistar!"

"How did you...happen to be captured?" I had now fully recovered from my first shock and was willing to accept the illusions of the wizard's image. After all, wizards were supposed to do fantastic, impossible things, cast spells, control minds, defeat armies—that was why they were called wizards.

"They came upon me in the courtyard, dressed as friends. Once inside the building, they said that my daughter was in their power and that I must surrender to their will or she would be killed. And before any of my personal staff and warriors could do a thing in my defense, they were cut down. It was impossible to get to my rooms to cast a spell. I attempted to overpower them with my *Inner Resources* but one of them came up from behind and knocked me unconscious. The next thing I knew I was waking up in this cell. I then became aware of a stranger in the cell next to mine. That was you." The figure shrugged. "But this challenge you have made to Lord Waja: I take it that you believe you can overcome this man—and then, being friends—or accepted as friends—you will leave?"

"No. Then I would stay until I found some way to rescue you and your daughter!" I spoke quite frankly.

The man studied me for a moment, as if considering the honesty of my words, then he nodded. "But this challenge of yours will not give you the results you so desire. Waja will call for the duel—but the swords will be stacked in his hands. You will be killed. Mark my warning!"

"I think not. I am an excellent swordsman—and anyway, there is nothing to lose, for he will probably kill me in any case. And your daughter and my...slave...will be his to use at will."

"You might be a good swordsman but so is this man of which Lord Waja speaks." The Wizard was thoughtful for a moment, tapping the point of his hooked nose. "If you could work your way to my Chambers of Wizardry...there is a potion which will give you strength and speed beyond the imaginings of men. But..." Again he shrugged, spreading his claw-like hands in the air. "You would not know which one to use."

"You could tell me—if you could give me direction," I suggested.

"I don't know. Let me think about it. Let me think about it." His image began to disappear, like the fading of firelight moving off into the distance.

"Wait! Could you not appear as you have now to me and point the way? If I were to get into the chambers you might be able to—direct me!"

The Wizard of Zorkada nodded, his form still fading. "We will see. We will see. For it is true, I could thus appear and lead your hand. Now that we have mental contact, it is possible. It is *possible*...but I can only hold my form for a short while—and if we do not have a prearranged meeting time—I will have to think of something."

With that his form disappeared.

I called after him but the Wizard did not answer.

Standing in the darkness of the cell I wondered what madness was attacking my senses. Then I realized that what I had seen could only be an illusion of my own mind—having no more substance or reality than a dream. But then...a wizard might be able to do such a thing, take such a form.

Suddenly I was very tired, very hungry.

Lying down on the hard stone floor, I leaned against the wall, stared into total darkness until sleep finally closed my eyes.

When I awakened I found it impossible to believe that I had not merely dreamed up the Wizard. I called out his name but my voice did not carry beyond the stone walls of my own cell.

I paced the floor in order to have something to do and keep my muscles exercised.

Time passed and I slept again. In the sleep came a dream of the Wizard moving through the castle like some shadowy form, gliding down misty dark hallways, moving through walls and doors, floating slightly above the air. I saw the image of Illa, sleeping, and the Shadow Wizard leaning over, gazing down at her. Then the dream passed and I was suddenly awake, sweat breaking out over my body.

My mouth was dry, the gnawing pit of my stomach cramped the muscles. I felt weak and exhausted. I slept after some time, only to wake again, sweating, even more weak and tired.

I got up, paced the floor, and wondered if they were going to leave me here to rot—die of starvation and thirst. Already much time had gone by since I'd had food or water.. I was weakened by the lack of substance in my body.

Suddenly I had the feeling that somebody was watching me. Cold sweat covered my body. It was as if invisible eyes were boring into my neck. Then I heard a voice which I immediately recognized.

"Thoris, they are coming for you. I can sense it. We don't have much time. I will try to be there to help. Watch for me! Don't be surprised to see me in the room with you and the others—but I will be visible only to you."

I turned but there was only darkness in the cell. I started to say something but the door clanged open to reveal two burly guards.

"You will come with us!" one of them announced.

As dimly lit as I knew the hall beyond to be, my eyes immediately began to hurt even from this semi-glow, so long had I been confined to total darkness. I squinted, moved forward. My body was weak, exhausted. My mouth felt as if the sun had been thrust into it. The lining of my stomach was raw, sick. For the first time the idea of using "magic" to win a duel seemed less disgusting and more necessary—for surely I was in no condition to give a fair showing.

"Come!"

I staggered forward and the two men roughly grabbed me.

"Here is the *mighty* swordsman we have been hearing about?" one laughed.

"He will not last long against the blade of Danj."

They shoved me along the hall, then up the stairs. Even before we reached the top I realized that death awaited me. Even against a poor swordsman I could not delay death for more than a couple of thrusts.

Then the two men pushed me through the open doorway and into the hall and finally to the throne room in which Lord Waja waited with some twenty warriors.

"Come, come!" encouraged Lord Waja, who stood in the middle of the room next to a slightly built man. "You will now have the chance to show off your great ability with the sword."

"I guess it's foolish to ask for food and drink?" I forced myself to stand firmly on both feet. Desperation had made it impossible to keep from asking the question which could only have one answer.

"Of course you may have food!" Lord Waja grinned; his expression contained a wicked secret. "It will be brought to you the moment you kill my Champion!" He motioned to the small slender man at his right. "This is Danj."

Danj was holding a long slim sword which he easily flashed through the air in an excellent display of skill, moving through half a dozen attacks which would have cut the average swordsman to pieces. It was impressive.

Even with my body fully toned, with good food and plenty of rest and exercise, this man would be a fairly good match. As it was, I had no chance at all.

86

Chapter eight

The danger of danj

Lord Waja moved to the throne and seated himself. "Let us begin. I am anxious for a little excitement. And please, Danj, take it easy. I want to be entertained. I'm not interested in seeing him murdered right off. Let's have some fun."

A warrior stepped swiftly to my side, extended a long wicked-looking sword of a design I had not seen before—other than the one which Danj held. It was far thinner than the normal long swords that are commonly issued to warriors, being at the base not as thick as a man's finger, and then tapering down to a needle point. Its balance, though, was quite light and my fingers wrapped themselves easily around the handle.

I swung the weapon through the air to test it and was pleased to discover it was very light and easy to control. I also learned quickly that the sword was handled much as the larger battle swords.

Just as Danj stepped forward, extending his blade, I saw a shimmering form suddenly appear a little behind him, against the far wall. For a moment I stood there, mouth opened, stunned. Even with the earlier warning, it was startling to see a man materialize in a room full of people and know that nobody else had seen him.

The image of the Wizard of Zorkada motioned toward Waja, then he glided up to the throne and moved behind it, disappearing from view.

At that moment I felt a sting of pain cut my left arm, then flash away. It was but a scratch, enough to command my attention.

"Come, man, fight!" laughed Danj, taking a stance with blade thrust forward, only a head from my chest. There was just the suggestion of red on its tip.

I raised my own weapon and carefully touched his. Hardly had the two blades made contact than Danj lunged. His movement was faster than eyes could follow. But even my sword had a speed all its own—moving automatically. The lightness of the weapon, coupled with long years of training, was going to hold off death only a few moments, but at least I could make some kind of showing. I parried the attack, parried again and again as the point leaped repeatedly at me.

Danj danced around my position like a bee flitting back and forth between flowers. His footwork was outstanding. He was merely playing a game. His thin lips were always spread with a grin of pleasure and contempt. His blade netted the air in front of me, weaving in and out, attempting to touch my naked chest. Several times I felt the razor pain as the point just scratched me.

I was fighting a totally defensive battle and it was clear right from the beginning that my strength could not last long. The only chance I had was to get to the chambers of Wizardry as Xalla had suggested; yet I hated to use magic to win a duel. But it was that or die—and the odds had been bluntly stacked in Danj's favor.

I started to back away from Danj and there was a murmur of contempt from the surrounding warriors.

"Come, come, man! Do not run!" Danj sneered. "Surely you are not afraid."

His point whipped out, touched my chest, slipped away. And again I felt his sword cut a line of pain across my chest. Three more times he drew blood. All I could do was stand there and vainly attempt to prolong my life—and get to the Chambers of Wizardry. His skill with the sword was amazing; he always brought the point just short of doing any real damage.

"You are no match for me!" Danj moaned, lowering his point in contempt of my swordsmanship.

In that moment I leaped forward, my sword lunging toward the man's unprotected heart. The blade ripped bloodily across his chest muscle just missing its intended target as the man had leaped aside.

The grin which had spread across his delicate face now wiped clean. "Now you die!"

Before he could attack I turned and ran to the throne.

My action so stunned all those in the room that nobody moved. I charged around the throne and into the small hall beyond. The form of Xalla shimmered in front of a huge door.

"This way, quick!" he called.

There were cries from the throne room behind me. Then footsteps sounded.

I rushed forward, knowing it was only a matter of half a dozen breaths before Danj would again be upon me. I moved to where the Wizard had been. He slipped into a huge high-ceilinged room.

"Close, bolt the door!" Xalla instructed.

"Where's the potion?" I slammed the huge metal door shut and slipped the bolt into place. I was already panting from exhaustion. All I wanted was to lie down and sleep—or eat—then sleep.

"This way!" Xalla pointed across the room, toward one of the many long benches which were cluttered with bottles and glasses, labeled in odd twirling golden symbols. "Hurry!"

I rushed along the bench, directly behind the image of Xalla.

"*That* bottle!" The Wizard pointed to a small bottle of greenish colored liquid. "Take a swallow of it. You will regain your strength—it is all I can do for you now!" As he spoke, he was slowly beginning to fade. First his image became transparent, then flickered. "The Gods be with you."

Then he was gone.

I heard fists pound against the large door. "Come out, you fool! You cannot escape death!"

I reached for the bottle, pulled the cork which stopped it, then for just a moment hesitated before taking a large swallow of the green colored contents.

The liquid tasted bitter and had an oily texture to it. For a moment nothing happened. I might have merely been drinking water. Then the substance suddenly spread through my nervous system and all of a sudden I felt an extraordinary charge of strength surge into my head. Everything brightened; light, the air itself, appeared to have tone that I could actually hear. The hunger was gone, the thirst assuaged.

I turned to the door, which seemed far more alive; the detail of the texture of the mental appeared to be sharpened. I was aware of every scratched detail, every imperfection of its surface. My senses seemed stronger than they had ever been before. Sounds had color, and color seemed to have sound. I could see the contractions of anger blaring through the door like visible force lines as the men behind it curse, talked among themselves.

It seemed that I merely thought about being at the door and opening it, and suddenly I was there, my hand on the latch. Immediately I was swinging the door open.

The half dozen men who had been slamming their fists against the door, shouting, suddenly froze, startled. It seemed as if their motions, their muscular movements, were slowed down; though this was not quite true. I could see every pore in their bodies, see every hair, yet at the same time watch the whole form of their body all at once. Thus it was with movement. I saw more detail, was aware of every muscle, every fraction of motion taking place. I was prewarned by the pressure of air when a muscle flexed for action.

Danj slowly fell back; his sword moved up as if in slow motion. I felt the muscles of his body contract, pressing the air in their effort. Everything he did appeared as if slowed to a fraction of what it had been before; though I knew that movement and time were the same as always. I was just able to define more detail.

I flicked out my blade. I cut lightly across Danj's harness, which supported the sword sheath. The leather sliced neatly apart and slid slowly to the floor to ring around his sandal covered feet.

As the man reacted in surprise, looked down at his fallen harness, I was already running down the hall. A moment later I stood in the throne room in front of Lord Waja.

"Where the Gods have you been?" Waja cried in rage, standing, his face suddenly deep red in color. "How *dare* you run off like that!"

I knew that it would easily be possible to kill the man right then. But I hesitated. Could I fight off this whole army unit? Would I not be cut down? How long would the drug last? I hesitated just long enough for Danj to return to the room. Then it was too late.

Danj's face was white, his eyes burned with hatred as they flashed at me.

"I'll kill you *fast* for that!" Danj screamed at the top of his lungs.

The man attacked, and I knew from experience that his movements would be extremely fast. Yet the sword seemed to glide slowly toward me, even though every muscle in the man's face, neck and body were tensed as if he were using every one of them to their fullest.

I neatly flicked his sword point away. It was as if he had just extended an arm outwards to lightly caress the air in front of him.

My blade moved, touched the man's cheek, drawing blood. I could have almost stated how many layers of skin had been cut through.

The temptation to kill him immediately was all but overwhelming but I resisted it. There was another more basic desire: to make a complete fool of him, as he had done with me.

This was cold murder; but his engaging me was just the same kind of murder. Now the sword had reversed and he was on the death end.

Instead of making the kill I took the defensive.

Danj attacked. I allowed his blade to come within a fraction of cutting my body, then knocked it lightly away. It was as if the man facing me were made of air, for his muscles gave no resistance to my blade.

91

"I'll kill you!" he cursed, renewing his efforts to do as he so violently promised.

But try as the man would, I easily tapped his weapon to one side or another. A couple of times I slapped my blade forcefully across his back and seat. Then I went so far as to merely touch his head lightly, tap his shoulder, brush his hair, not once hurting him, not once drawing blood. It was a delightful little game.

He grew tense, his face drained of all color and took on the balanced whiteness of terror. And finally the sword in his hand extended toward me and I flicked it to one side; it flew out of his grasp, clattered across the floor and hit the far wall.

My point leaped out for the man's exposed throat. I touched the flesh, then drew back. This was cold-blooded murder.

Danj stood there as if made of hard stone, his features etched sharply into solid ridges. Then as if having been pushed from behind, he began to topple. The next moment he hit the ground, face first, and did not move after that.

Everybody in the room went silent for a long time. Nobody moved. I looked from one to another, then finally turned my gaze to Lord Waja, who was standing there like marble.

"Well, will my sword do? Will you buy it now?" I smiled frozenly, knowing how easy it would be to kill him and defeat the warriors in the room. But I could not resist playing my little charade first.

"But...but how? You had not had food for days! How could you have defeated Danj? It's the magic of the Wizard! He is behind this!" Lord Waja stood; his face grew deep red. "It was not a fair fight!"

"You did not intend it to be fair!" I observed casually. "If I had had food and drink for the last few days I could have bested him in any case."

"You cheated!" he screamed accusingly.

"It does not really matter. I defeated your best swordsman. I offered my sword in your services!" I bowed, holding back little of my contempt or anger.

"Take him! *Take him!"* Waja screamed at the top of his voice, all but jumping up and down in fury.

A dozen men leaped forward. But their actions were too slow. I met their attack one at a time. As my blade sank into the second warrior I felt my strength suddenly begin to slip away, like sand drifting from the top section of an hourglass. The world around me was beginning to speed up. The movements of the Vistar swordsmen were more deadly, less distinct. Normalcy was returning.

I immediately attempted to kill off as many as possible while there was still strength in me. My sword flashed into the body of one man, then cut across the neck of another.

"Stop! Stop! *Stop!"* came Lord Waja's screamed command. "Stop at once before all of you fools are killed!"

The men drew happily back away from my blade, relief marking their grim faces. It was obvious that they had no desire to continue a battle which offered only instant death.

Inwardly I gave out a sigh of relief. Another few moments and I would have been quickly overpowered by force of numbers—and no doubt killed. The timing had been almost too perfect.

"Your sword!" Lord Waja hissed, his face a controlled mask, "is too great to be stopped. I will take your services rather than kill such a skilled sword."

"My price is high!" I countered. "I wish my slave returned and—"

"Don't go too far! I will have you killed rather than have you dictate to me. Your slave is my property...until I decide I can trust you! You will come into my service without conditions—as a common warrior-at-arms!" he cried harshly, fists doubled up at his side, face contorted with rage. "Do you understand?"

I just managed to keep from swaying as I bowed. My weakness was now all but overpowering. "I will serve you well, my Lord."

"Take him away. Take him away! Give him sleeping quarters!"

"And food," I suggested.

"And food!" Lord Waja cursed.

"And drink," I pushed, wondering just how afraid Lord Waja was of my sword.

"And drink," he cursed between clenched teeth.

A couple of men who had just been fighting with me, stepped forward.

"Come," the tallest ordered.

I followed, not once revealing my weakness. Every step seemed an effort almost beyond the ability of my muscles. Yet as we moved out of the throne room and went down the hall, outside into the courtyard, and then to one of the small doors which opened on the ground floor, I managed to keep the appearance up of still having at least normal strength. All this time the two guards had remained at a safe distance of several heads, as if still afraid of the sting of my blade, which I had continued to hold.

"You will sleep here with the rest of us," one of the men announced as we stepped into a large narrow room meant to sleep warrior units. On each wall were lined bunks and racks for weapons and harness. There was that about the room and its arrangement which seemed very familiar and homelike; for I had been a warrior all my adult life.

"Where can I get food and drink?" I quickly demanded.

"It will be brought. Take an unoccupied bunk. There you will discover the proper harness of a warrior at arms. You'll do as the unit officer instructs if you don't want trouble." The man looked sternly at me.

But his fellow managed a friendly smile. "You are truly a mighty swordsman."

"Mighty or not," the other grumbled, "he will do his duties as all of us. Just as he is told!"

With that the two men turned and left.

I stepped across the room to a bunk which had a leather harness and weapons hanging on a peg in the wall. It looked unoccupied. As I lay down on the hard leather cot a stirring seemed to crackle in the air. Immediately I knew who it was.

"I see you survived!" the voice of Xalla, the Wizard of Zorkada, whispered at my side.

94

I turned, saw him standing there over me, his wise old eyes filled with an expression I could not fathom. It was not warm with friendliness but there was a sense of fellowship and calculating self-interest—and something else that I could not label.

"I'm glad to see you still alive, Thoris of Rota. You will now be in a far better position to serve our common interests!" He spoke impersonally, his voice that of a man talking to another whom he cannot quite trust.

"I would be dead but for your help!"

"True. True. But you are a skilled swordsman. It would be a great sight to see you and Danj fight it out on equal terms—or better yet under the Spell of Power." He shrugged, philosophically. "But such seems not to be written in the Heavens!"

"I must find out how Illa is!" My legs slipped over the side of the cot.

"The girls are fine—in the tower, together. I have visited my daughter several times in the past days. Your...Illa...is aware of our plans. I will let her know that you are safe—so far. But from here on you must play it carefully. Do not swiftly trust Lord Waja—or this swordsman, Danj, for he will willingly run a sword through you at the first possible moment—if for no other reason than to prove he is better than you."

The sound of footsteps came from the other end of the long room.

I turned to see a man walking towards us, carrying a tray on which sat a plate of food and a large metal cup.

Xalla grinned, whispered, "He cannot hear me—so do not worry. Ignore the fact that I am here."

The Vistarian stepped to my side, laid the tray down and then without so much as a greeting or goodbye, turned and quickly left the room.

"It looks good!" Xalla exclaimed. "I would give away half my secrets for a meal like this right now."

"Have you not been fed?" I looked up at the old man's shimmering image.

"No—they will get around to it—if they plan on letting me live. You must discover their plans before making any move. And then you must move as fast as possible."

"How do you live?" I was now looking at the food in front of me. It was the first real meal I had seen since leaving the ship *Vayis* during the storm—since then it had been fruits; a diet unsuited for a warrior.

"I have my powers, my *Inner Resources!* But they will not last forever. I must go now. But I will return from time to time. Discover what you can about Lord Waja's plans. He is no doubt under war orders—it should not be hard to discover what they are." As he spoke, the image of his form was quickly fading away.

I ignored all but the food in front of me now. There was a large piece of cold meat, a few long root-like orange-colored vegetables, which I had never seen before, and a cup of liquid the color of leather with little bubbles which kept trickling up to the surface.

I quickly drank some of the liquid and discovered that it had a pleasant but slightly salty taste. I took the meat in hand and started slowly, anxiously to eat. Never had a meal tasted so good as this one. I kept sipping from the large cup and finally when I was finished eating I lay on the bunk. My head was now spinning; the liquid was some kind of Ijan beer, I learned later, and had created its pleasant effects on my tired body.

I lay there half in a dream world, for the first time in days feeling human again. But as thought centered more logically, I realized that there was no cause to feel safe or comfortable.

Princess Illa and myself were prisoners; there was no way to leave the castle of Xalla. And even if we were to leave, passage through the lands of Zorkada and Jorjos could prove fatal without help.

No, I reasoned sleepily, I would have to find some way to succor the Wizard and his daughter, and hope that with their help I might find my way to the land of Andus, where Dasha ruled in the name of Muda, God-Lord of Haldolen.

CHAPTER NINE

THE WIZARD'S PACT

It seemed I hardly closed my eyes before a hand was roughly shaking me.

"Come man, wake up! Duty time!" The voice was irritated, harsh.

I opened my eyes, immediately sat up, swung my legs over the side of the bed.

The man who stood in front of me was fully armed with long and short sword, knife, and was holding a crossbow—which takes far greater personal skill to use—though I had learned of the crossbow and knew that it was in use in some of our colonies. The man before me was a warrior-at-arms, with rank nine printed on the front of his yellow uniform. His features were chiseled in square lines; a beard pointed the bottom of his chin.

"You are to assist me!" he announced. "I am Baya, and since you are a warrior of the tenth rank in the armies of Vistar, you will do my bidding! I'm on gate watch and you are to relieve me. Go to the Officer in charge of the gate and report in. He will instruct you as to your duties."

I started to object, then decided against it. As far as I was concerned it did not really matter what duties they forced me into. During the next rest period I could do a little investigating of my own. But until then it might be possible to pick up information.

I reached for the harness hung on the wall peg, then looked at the other warrior. "Have there been any signs of resistance?"

As I expected, the man assumed I knew more than I did. "None. The Zorkadians are cowards. Without their Wizard they have lost the claws that kept us great Vistars from conquering them. Now they quiver in fear!" He laughed heartily.

"What has happened to the mighty Wizard?"

"He's seen his day! He is locked up below. I don't think Lord Waja knows exactly what to do with the *creature*. So he waits. Xalla will need great magic to keep from dying of starvation and thirst. Lord Waja doesn't know if he should use the old Wizard or forget that the *thing* exists!"

"A hard decision, I must admit!" I offered gravely, starting to walk down the long row of bunks to the front door. "I'll see you later, Baya."

"Keep a sharp sword alert!" The man had already stepped to a bunk across the room. He sat down. "Don't fall asleep at the guard post or you will be killed by our Lord Master!"

As I stepped into the courtyard it was difficult to realize that they gave me this sort of total freedom of the castle, and weapons, too! It would seem so easy to free the Wizard now. But that might be exactly what Lord Waja awaited. For the moment he was impressed with the flash of my blade and no doubt had his private plans for me.

I moved to the large gate in front of the castle's drawbridge. There were several guards standing there at attention, their hands resting at each thigh, just touching short and long sword sheaths, eyes straight ahead.

There was one man dressed in a yellow-orange cape, who was obviously the officer in charge. He paced back and forth, hands clasped behind his back. When I approached him, he turned, glared at me.

"You are the new man?"

"Yes, great warrior," I offered, hoping that would be the salute-of-rank he expected.

"You will stand there, next to the drawbridge, watching the approach." He pointed toward the controls of the gate and drawbridge.

"If the trumpets blare from the towers, you will immediately raise the gate." He stared at me as if attempting to read my mind. "Do you understand?"

"Yes, my officer."

I moved to the gate, took up my position like the others, but faced toward the surrounding jungle. A short time later another warrior came and stood to my right.

Evening slowly settled down upon the land and finally Fahda the Sun lowered into its western resting place for the night. Black sky folded around the world and the stars twinkled down upon us. The soft murmur of wind through the trees mixed with the coughs and screams of savage night creatures of the jungle.

The man next to me suddenly spoke softly.

"You are the warrior who defeated Danj in the duel, is that not true?" The fellow's voice was filled with awed admiration.

"We fought. I am still breathing," was my simple answer.

"You must be a mighty warrior for Danj is the greatest of all swordsman! I would be careful if I were you, for he prided himself on the title he held. He can be a dangerous enemy. Be careful."

"Surely he would not have me cut down without a single chance to fight in my own defense." The conversation was soft enough so that the words would not go far beyond ourselves.

"Surely he *would*—by pitting you against a foe nobody could defeat. Maybe on a hunt for food he will see that there is an *accident.*"

"Why do you tell me this?"

"Nobody likes Danj! He is a great sword, and we are proud to have such a great man in our units, but he is a bully and uses his sword power over the rest of us. He is not popular."

I asked: "How long are we to stay here in the castle of the Wizard?"

"We do not know. I have heard we await the surrender of Hallis, Ruler of Zorkada. Our mission here was to capture the Wizard and send a message to the Zorkadian ruler to surrender the lands for which we have fought so long and hard."

His voice changed, becoming tinted with curiosity. "Where do you come from?"

"Nowhere that you would know of. I wander. Surely there are others much like myself who come through this fine country of yours."

"Not many. There are a few. Everybody has heard of such men who seek adventure on their own terms. How they live out their first Four-Seasons I don't know." There was a shrug in the man's voice.

"We survive with our wits and swords. Though I must admit that your Lord is a harsh man. Not everybody is as harsh as he. Most Lords will hire a sword arm without question. I would be dead but for my skill with the sword. And not be here, talking to you, I might add." I was fast becoming an expert liar.

"And would not have brought shame to Danj, either." The man suddenly whispered: "Quiet, now!"

The officer in charge of our detail stepped close, asked: "How are things, men?"

"Fine, my officer," the other guard quickly stated in a sharp, military manner.

"Well?"

That last was directed at me, and I repeated the salute of, "Fine, my officer," and the man left.

Further conversation was directed by me, "I would assume that conversation while on guard is against the rules."

"No. Only that one should not let the officer in charge become aware of your conversation."

"But surely he knows we are talking."

"Of course. Naturally. But it is considered better for guards to talk than go to sleep. But they must not talk too loudly and embarrass the guard officer. We talk, but softly."

Silence followed for a moment, then I asked: "I know little of the lands in which I find myself. Would you tell me something about Jorjos?"

The man said: "Well, we are a group of city-states, each having many lands. We grow food, we hunt, we war

among ourselves, but when outsiders come—like the Haldolen armies—we are strong! The Haldolenians are careful to
leave us alone, for many Four-Seasons ago we gave battle to
their exploring ships and gave warning that we did not want
anything to do with them. We wish to be left alone. Each
city-state is governed by its own Ruler, but in times of mutual dangers, we band tightly together and nobody could pull
us apart! The Haldolenians wish every piece of land they can
get their greedy hands on. We wish to be left alone. The
Haldolen Empire will never have our Jorjos without a battle
to the death—a war which might someday come about, and
many will thus be killed. Their colonies which surround the
land of Jorjos leave us totally alone, mainly because of the
high mountains which surround Jorjos on the landward side.
What else is there to know about us?"

"What about your Gods?"

"Gods are for the dead—not the living!"

"Surely you do homage to the Gods!"

"Only upon the death of a brave warrior—or a rela-
tive. We have the Temple of the Dead, which makes much
profit in death. Then it is that you will give great homage to
the Gods and the priests of the Temple of the Dead will eat
well that day! They rob us! But...one must send your loved-
one to a happy life beyond. But that's all. Gods rule the af-
ter-life, not the living-life—other than those Temple priests
who *make* a living out of sending us on our way to the lands
beyond death. Gods have put us here to struggle with the
world around us, as we see fit. It is up to us what kind of life
we have. The Rules, the Laws of Nature, are here and we
must fight as best we can. Cold will kill, fire will burn and
kill. Therefore you must learn how to survive. A sword will
kill—so you avoid the death-point of such a weapon. Cut the
flesh and blood pours out—and loss of blood will bring
death. There are many rules like, don't fall down the slide of
life for a long fall will crush your body. We study the rules
as children, taught by Learners, who have learned much that
there is to know from the Searchers and Wizards. The
Searchers seek knowledge of the world around us; the Wizards use this knowledge combined with the secrets of their
magic art to bring the Gods forth in the real world! And

Therefore Wizards have powers not of this world. Yet, they are as human as you and I! And they can die! They merely know great secrets of magic."

"This world beyond life you talk of, what is it?" I inquired, fascinated. "In Haldolen we do not think about any life after death, for how could there be such?"

"We all go to another life beyond that of this world. We live with the Gods and we learn all the real secrets of living. In that place, beyond our world-life, is perfection. One can fall from a tall wall, can run a sword through his heart, can lose all blood in his body, cut his neck off, insult an officer, touch a goddess, and nothing will befall him other than what he so desires. Surely you know of the Place Beyond!"

"I know nothing of it, for I am a simple wanderer— searching for truth, one might say. But I have never found it."

"What truth have you searched for?"

"There is not time to explain," I quickly stated. "Tell me, are we far from the city of Zorkada?"

"City of Zorkada? There is no such place. There is Zorkada. There we are now standing. There is the city of Hallis. Is that what you mean?"

"Yes, I would imagine. Where the Ruler of Zorkada lives."

"We are but a day's journey by foot." He laughed. "You know nothing of our lands."

"I know little, it is true. And very little of your Gods who do not help you in life but only give you an after-death life...I can hardly believe there is life after death. But, then, I have never really considered it."

"Vass, our great prophet, has said that no man can conceive of his own death—the end of all thought and being. His thoughts on the subject are involved—but he believes there are Gods and that there is a life after death. Surely you don't believe that when you die you will exist no more? Think about it. Try to conceive of your own end. No sleep with dreams to haunt you, no thoughts. Nothing! Just: the end of all!"

His voice seemed to shudder.

We grew silent. For a long time I found my thoughts frozen to the idea which the nameless warrior had offered. The concept of total and complete death was hard to swallow; impossible to imagine—yet surely seemed most logical in a beautiful way. After all, I lived, I breathed, I thought— so I could not conceive of my end—for what purpose would I have been born if just to live for a short time and then return to the nothing from which I had come? Yet, why live forever? They are questions, I might add, which I have not answered to this day—nor have all the Wise Men of Haldolen given an answer to them.

And so the long watch, half a day long, drifted by. When over, my muscles were strained, even though I was used to such duty, since for many Seasons it was all I had done in the service of my Goddess of Rota, protecting her Temple.

When Baya came to the guard post and said to me, "You can go now," it was early in the morning.

I had learned some important facts from both Baya and this guard and now would use this information. First I had to contact Xalla.

As I stepped across the courtyard, intent on going into the main hallway of the Castle which led to the throne room and the dungeons below, my thoughts were muddled from the long watch of night. My attention was completely centered upon finding some way to rescue the Wizard, if all else failed.

Suddenly I felt someone bump against my shoulder. A loud cry of anger sounded.

My eyes immediately focused, nerves coiled muscles, ready for instant combat.

Danj, hand on the hilt of his sword, eyes blazing, was standing in front of me. There were two other warriors at his side. A slow grin played on his lips.

"We meet again—but without the Wizard's poison to give you supernatural powers!" The sword started to lift from the sheath.

I reacted, using every muscle in my body to create a display which would not only be unexpected but demoralizing. My right hand flashed to the sheathed sword. Before

103

anybody had moved, I had the sword in hand, extended towards Danj. The man suddenly paled.

"What's the meaning of this?" He strained closer, all but ignoring the point of my sword.

One of the two warriors grabbed hold of his arms. "Careful, Danj."

The other warrior nodded. "You don't know that the Wizard's spell is not still in effect...and Lord Waja would not like you fighting with him again!"

Danj relaxed. There was a moment of silence before the man smirked. It was a dangerous grin that spread those thin lips wide across crooked teeth. "I am glad to see you are an alert swordsman. Someday we might cross swords again—but I want everything to be equal!"

"Equally on your side only?" I offered, sneering.

The man's face turned dark and his right hand edged to the sword's hilt. Then he seemed to think better of it. "There will come a time when you are not so cocky, warrior, *and that might be sooner than you think!*"

With that, Danj turned and walked away, the two men at his side.

I watched him disappear into the small doorway with the other two close behind.

Danj was not frightened off so easily. No doubt he was fearful that the magic of Xalla I had used to win an unequalled match was still in effect.

I turned and stepped into the corridor upon whose walls were painted the battling warriors and the wizard-image at the end.

Just as I approached the door which led to the dungeons, the throne room swung open and Lord Waja stepped out. He paused upon seeing me.

"What are you doing here, warrior?" he demanded curtly.

"Am I not allowed here?"

"Not unless so ordered. Get out at once, before I have you killed. Gifted as you might be with the sword, you will not be able to fight off my archers' arrows. So, beware, warrior!" He waved a thin finger in my face.

Immediately I turned and left the corridor.

104

Standing in the courtyard once more, I turned with hesitation and moved to the left, starting up the first staircase.

The Castle of Xalla the Wizard was a huge place with many floors and rooms. It was only a short distance to the second floor and a ramp ran along the building, with many doors opening to the courtyard below. I had stepped along the ramp for some ten heads from the staircase when a crackling old voice softly whispered in my ear: "Continue down this way until you come to the last room—it is empty, and there we can talk about our plans without being disturbed."

I did as instructed without once looking back to see if the Wizard of Zorkada was following me.

Upon opening the door I felt a jolt of surprise for the Wizard sat there on a small bunk in the room.

"Close the door, Thoris of Rota!" Xalla commanded. He was sitting with arms folded on his chest, eyes probing up at me like a wise old seer, a strange, amusing twist on his thin lips. "Well, now, my warrior, tell me what you have discovered!"

"They are demanding the surrender of lands over which your war has been fought. They plan on starving you, I would imagine. They believe you are totally in their power!" I fired the statements at him like a stream of arrows shot from a powerful bow. Only on the last did he show any reaction.

"They have a surprise awaiting them!" he cackled, face distorted into an etching of wrinkles.

"But what can you do?"

"It is not what I can do, my boy, but what *you* can do for me!" His eyes snapped up to mine, then those leathery lips quivered as the sound of evil laughter issued from them. "There are many potions in my chamber of Wizardry—there are many others than what you have already been exposed."

The Wizard grew serious for a moment. I started to say something but he quickly raised a knotted finger, shaking it. His lips pursed. All at once Xalla stood, slowly turned. "There are things, my boy, which only Wizards learn! There are great magic wonders in every day life that the common man does not know. There are gods and devils, there are un-

105

known things of graves, unknown things of the wind and airs and dirt, which can all be combined into a concoction only a Wizard of Great Learning can use to an advantage. There are tricks and tricks, ones which fall upon each other in such a confusion that only a Master can twist them apart. You can learn one trick and a Wizard will flip it around and get another effect. Fire can turn to water, water into flames. Lead to gold. A stick can turn into a snake—and then back again into a lifeless stick. Light can come from a small metal wire, burning bright, to flash away all dark. Day from night!" He waved his arms in the air around him, the robe rustled realistically in response, as if he were truly in the room with me.

"There are ways to make a man's mind turn soft, ways to make his mind a giant. Ways to make flight possible! I can open your mental world, as quickly and easily as your physical world was speeded up. I can open wonders to you that are undreamed by your puny mind. The Universe in all its vastness—the stars, like our sun, will speed into your mind and you will count all the planets in the sky, plant all the stars in the day sky.

"But..." He shrugged, spread his hands out wide, shrugged again. "But...I would be a fool to open all those doors to you. There are doors behind which only *I* can see, can understand, can go. Their dark mysteries are only for me to comprehend and use. But..."

He moved closer to me, standing just under my chin, his scrawny neck seeming to strain, the long white beard striking my stomach. *"You*, my boy, Thoris the Mighty, will learn the means to conquer all of the Vistars, single-handed. But it will be dangerous. You might easily be killed. You could surely be killed if caught before you are ready for battle!

"It will not be easy—and the doors which will open to you will seem horrifying, chilling the very centers of your bones with a terror you cannot see—cannot even imagine. I will open but a few of my Chambers to you, directing your hand, so that you will succeed where all others might fail." His eyes lit brightly; their centers seemed to flash gold, then flaming red like the hot coals of a fire. "You will help me defeat the Vistars and send them away!"

106

Immediately I could see that the Wizard of Zorkada was totally helpless without my hand to direct his magic. He would die, and was afraid of death—he would never leave the cell in the dungeons if I did not help him; and it was quite possible that were I to take the Vistars' side, freedom for Illa and myself might be offered in reward.

"I will help. Xalla, on one condition. You will free Illa and myself and you will give us passage to the lands of Andus to the South and East of here, for that was where we were headed when I first met and rescued your daughter. I have friends who lived there."

"Your reward will be complete—and all that you wish will be heaped upon you. Riches, position, anything you name! I will so promise!"

He reached a hand out towards mine.

I hesitated, drew back, for surely an image, a projection could not touch my flesh. Then his hand surged forward and "gripped" mine in a most realistic manner. There was a slight tingling sensation, totally different from actual physical contact. Yet it was obvious that in some strange mental way he had managed to touch me.

"The pact is sealed," Xalla announced. "None can break the promise made. It is sealed in Wizard's Spirit! Even if I so desired, I could not but keep my promise.

"Come, I will lead you to my Chambers of Wizardry, and we will concoct a magic that will chill the very bones of the Vistars who dared to match wits with the great Wizard of Zorkada!"

"But, how will we get into your Chambers? There are guards, and Lord Waja himself ordered me out of that part of the Castle!" I told him.

"Come, follow me—there are ways of which this Lord Waja knows nothing!" He motioned with his hand toward the opposite wall. "Come—press against the wall—*here*—and you will find a corridor that will lead down through the walls of my castle. I will show you the way from there."

CHAPTER TEN

GHOST OF XALLA

After stepping without hesitation to where the Wizard had disappeared, I reached out and pressed the wall where he had indicated. A heartbeat later a panel slipped away, revealing a dark, looming narrow passageway which went downwards, following the line of the wall.

As I stepped into the passage, the panel closed automatically behind me. I waited, expecting to find myself in total darkness. Then slowly a dim glow seemed to well from the walls themselves. It was just enough light to see by.

Slowly I stepped down along the narrow passageway, which had just enough width to make movement unrestricted. Two men could not easily pass each other here.

There was a silence to this corridor world, in which I now moved, that seemed uncanny and forbidding. Only the hollow echoing of my footsteps broke the quiet.

The steps seemed to go on and on at first, then finally they leveled off and I was standing at the beginning of a long hallway that had small panels on each side every six to ten heads. The castle was apparently laced with such passages, letting one go secretly from one room to another at will. I could easily imagine the horror of a house guest who looked around to discover another in the room where there was no visible way of entering other than the front door. The Wizard had, no doubt, had some fun in his time. Hopefully all his magic was not so shallowly simple.

I wondered how long I must continue without help from Xalla. Suddenly his image appeared in front of me, just a few heads away. He stood before one of the panels.

108

"Here are my Chambers of Wizardry!" he announced. "Careful. First we must check to see that nobody is in the room."

The panel pulled slowly back as I pressed its surface and a moment later I stepped into a vacant room cast in deep shadows of darkness. It was hard to see anything beyond ten heads. But the Wizard quickly solved the problem of light.

"Take this, twist the handle," he instructed, pointing to a bulb-like object attached to the wall just right of the Chamber's secret entrance.

When I twisted the small handle at its bottom, the bulb flashed with bright light. Startled, I cringed back for just an instant, then relaxed. After all, this was Wizard's magic, and there was nothing to be afraid of just so long as I was on the Wizard's side.

"Here," Xalla instructed softly, "over here, Thoris the Mighty, you will become the most shadowy warrior in the castle!" A chuckle sounded from his aged lips and he doubled over in obvious delight with himself. "You will become a shadow, without a shadow—a darkness which cannot be seen, a shadow without form, without substance. You will move about the castle of Xalla and none will perceive you other than myself. You will be in darkness in the dark, light in the light. All will be as blind men in your presence." He doubled over again with laughter.

I stood there in the dimly lit Chambers of Wizardry, mystified, watching the ancient man convulse with delight and pleasure. Finally, Xalla masterfully gained control of himself, turned to face me.

"You will become invisible! I should have thought of that before. It is perfect. You will be invincible. None shall harm you, other than blind chance which might push you against a naked blade. I have seen men go insane when faced with an Invisible Warrior! You will have the power of life and death, sanity and madness over all. You will chase the Vistars from my castle."

"But how can you make me invisible?" I inquired.

"The Cloak of Invisibility. The Spell which will cast your light into another world. Your body will be here but the light which reflects against it is dissipated into another di-

109

mension—as will the light of those objects that touch the warmth of your body."

Xalla squeezed his beard, thoughtfully. "I've always wondered what those who live in that other dimension must think when one's light is projected into their world. Probably they think it is a ghost!" He chuckled at that. "Now, in here—in this compartment—you will discover the necessary powders. I will instruct you."

I opened the compartment in front of which the Wizard of Zorkada had been standing and found myself facing row upon row of small bottles filled with powders, rocks, sands, of such varying colors that for a moment I was dazzled by the sight.

Xalla began pointing.

"Here—there, and there, and here, and that one, and this one, there, and, oh, yes, don't forget that one, for this greenish powder will give duration. Very important! Otherwise you will pulsate, appearing and disappearing. And this misty blue compound, that will give the ability to control your invisibility. And the yellow one will give it a time-control. A pinch of that substance for every one-thirtieth of a day." His hands had been flying, pointing, indicating, all but drawing the bottles out from their shelves, moving with such speed that it was almost impossible to keep up with his momentum, but finally ten bottles, containing powders and grainy substances of different colors, were standing on the bench in front of us.

The Wizard indicated a large empty bottle on the bench, instructed me to fill it with water. "Over there, in the sink, you will find all the water you need. Just turn that lever, the water will come from the exposed pipe."

The sink was about two heads square and one head deep. A round pipe extended over it with a lever at its side. I pulled the lever and water suddenly started pouring out of the pipe and into the sink.

Such wonders!

I filled the large bottle and then returned to the work bench.

"Now, a pinch of that, two of this, a little of that—not so much! That's better. And some of that—just pour—

enough! A sprinkle of that and then a pinch of this one." And so on, until all ten had been added to the water which kept changing colors with every new addition. By the time something from each bottle had been added, the water was once again clear, sparkling as if it were made of diamonds.

"And now...over there! You will find a red liquid, this you mix with the black of night potion over there. And then pour them into your invisibility mixture. Then you will have all you need for the total defeat of the Vistars."

I had just finished mixing the red and black liquid, which had taken on a misty blue color, when suddenly the huge double doors of the Chamber of Wizardry burst open and half a dozen warriors filed in.

"I thought I heard noise here!" one said.

Another demanded: "What are you doing here?"

I turned, and before any could guess my intentions, I had leaped for the doors, slamming and bolting them closed. I drew my sword and faced the six warriors in the narrow confines of an aisle between rows of benches. In this manner they could not approach me more than two at a time.

In my years of experience with the sword I had faced more than one warrior in a single moment of combat; I knew how to keep two swords busy; but right then the odds were against me.

No word was spoken; it was as if verbal sound were limited to grunts and wordless curses of fighting men engaged in battle. The grate of swords escaping their sheaths was the only indication of the death which would soon fall upon the room.

My sword flicked out in a feint to the man on my left, then crossed right to engage the other's sword. My sole purpose was to drink blood quickly, cut down the odds before they had recovered from their surprise. The ring of steel on steel was like a clanging gong in the room.

Again I feinted, making the same move as before, but this time my sword plunged forward, deep into the body of the second man, swung quickly out and parried an attack from the left. Before one of the men behind could move up to engage me, I had carved an ugly, bloody wound across the naked chest of the second warrior.

My blade moved into a series of attacks and feints, flicking out like a whip, parrying, attacking, creating a net of death before me. Another warrior fell, a fourth crumbled before my point.

The two remaining men stood there frozen for but a moment then started backing up. But I attacked, lunging forward, my blade knocking their weapons to one side, dancing out, touching a chest, cutting across a neck. The two fell. I finished off the wounded man, then sheathed my blade, surveying the six dead bodies.

I returned to the mixing of my concoction of magical invisibility.

As I reached for the bottle which contained the misty blue mixture, I heard the Wizard's voice wheeze joyfully next to me: "You are truly a mighty swordsman!"

"Luck was with me. Only luck!"

"Luck a little, skill a lot. I have never seen such a display of swordsmanship. But enough. On with the mixture. Combine the two liquids, and then quickly drink down as much of it as you can hold. At least one beaker full!" He indicated the beaker—which was the size of a Muda Beer glass—in which I should combine the two liquids.

Then I quickly did as instructed and watched with fascination as the liquids started to foam, then smoke. The smoke curled up like some blue misty haze, long white fingers twisting toward the high ceiling.

"Drink! Fast! While it is in action!" Xalla cried, alarmed.

I drank, gulping the amazingly warm potion. It had a salty taste, but otherwise seemed not other than water.

"There, the deed is done. You will have but half a day! But it should be enough to bring terror to the Vistars!" Xalla announced. "Just remember that you can *will* visibility back. You can do this merely by thinking hard about it; very hard indeed. For in your drug is a mind enlarging base which makes it possible to control the rhythm of your body; to bring it back to normal. But once visible you will remain so. You will have to return for another drink of the potion. Do you feel any different?"

I shook my head, mystified.

"It takes a moment or so. You will not become invisible to yourself—you will notice no real difference. You will simply be transparent to all those who gaze upon you—totally nonexistent! Your harness, weapons, all will go from visible sight because they will feel the warmth of your body; all you touch will visually disappear. Nobody will see anything other than that which is around you, beyond you." The Wizard's image was shimmering. "Now it is up to you, I grow tired. This has been most exhausting and I am all but a breath away from death, Thoris. If you fail, I fear we will never meet again. So...this is—goodbye! And good luck!"

As his vision faded completely, I felt totally alone. No sense of change had taken place, there was no physical awareness that my body might have suddenly stopped being visible. I gazed at my hands and of course they were still there.

But a shock came when I looked at one of the bottles in front of me in which a man's vision might surely reflect. I attempted to find my form there but there was no indication that a man stood in front of it. Instead I could make out the distorted details of the table directly behind me.

Just then there was a pounding on the door. A voice yelled.

I didn't answer, but moved slightly forward, unlatched the door and slowly swung in open.

A guard stood there, sword in hand. It seemed to take him a couple of moments to notice the dead warriors lying on the floor. Then a curse burst from his lips. He surged forward.

I slipped a foot out in front of him and he tumbled over, falling on his face.

Leaping to his feet, sword extended, he jerked around, bewildered and then frightened.

Silently I slipped my knife from its sheath and carefully stepped close. When I was within a head of the frightened warrior, I gently pricked his shoulder, then caught the edge of his blade with my knife, holding it back.

He screamed as if mortally wounded; then dropped his sword, turned and ran from the room, arms flaying in the air.

A grim smile played on my lips. I could imagine his utter terror. Oddly enough I felt no guilt. I must rid the castle of Vistars—and free Illa and return her to Haldolen and safety. All else was of little importance.

I knew that the warrior would no doubt return with others. I smiled to myself as I started moving the bodies of the six dead Vistar warriors. I dragged them one at a time to the wall panel, which easily opened at my touch. I had hidden five of them when footsteps sounded down the hall. Hurriedly I grabbed the sixth man, fairly stuffed him beyond the panel, and then closed it—just it time.

I turned to see an officer and three high-ranking warriors step into the room, escorting the terrified man who had left the room but a few moments before.

"Where are the dead?" the officer demanded.

One of the warriors pointed. "There—look!" He was indicating a trail of blood which led to the panel in the wall.

I mentally cursed myself and the Gods of Haldolen for having not thought of that; then I realized it did not really matter.

"But it stops at the wall," the other warrior said in a trembling voice.

The officer nodded. "A secret room. That's where your *ghost* is!"

He turned to the white-faced warrior who had first come into the room. Slapping the man, he cried: "How dare you interrupt me in the middle of my duties!"

"But...it was a ghost!" the other managed.

Determined to help the poor fellow, I tapped the officer on the shoulder, said: "It is a ghost, like he said." Then on inspiration added: "The ghost of Xalla, Wizard of Zorkada."

Then I retreated before the other could accidentally touch me.

The man leaped back so fast that he almost brushed my shoulder.

"Who was that?" he fairly screamed.

"It is I!" my voice rang out disembodiedly.

The man leaped at where I had been but contacted only empty air for I had stepped to one side.

114

"Go—go! Go from here!" I commanded. "Or you will die a terrible horrible unnatural death."

The officer recovered, slightly. "No ghost will frighten the Vistars. A ghost can do no harm!"

I had to admire the man' courage. But then, the Vistars had gone up against the Wizard of Zorkada before.

I moved close to the man, reached out and brushed his cheek with my hand. He turned a chalk white, his lips opened, trembled, a sound of choked horror rumbled from his throat. I then slapped his face, hard, then hit him in the middle of the stomach—not too hard. My efforts were designed to frighten and make the point that a ghost could do quite a bit of harm.

He fairly ran out the door, followed by the others, who cast frightened glances over their shoulders.

I heard the officer scream that a guard be posted on the door. Then his running footsteps faded away.

Luckily the man had not guessed about the corridors which traced through the castle of Xalla, and apparently believed he could contain a "ghost" in a single room. I quickly went to the panel, opened it and stepped over the dead bodies of the fallen Vistar warriors. Now I worked my way along the corridor to another panel some twenty heads away. I gently pressed the panel, and found myself looking into a lighted corridor. There wasn't anybody within sight so I stepped out and quickly closed the panel behind me. I was none too fast. A couple of warriors entered the hallway.

I watched them pass by as if I did not exist.

For a few moments I stood there, undecided what to do, for no plan of action had solidified. I must get Illa free but in order to do this and get passage through Zorkada safely, I must also rid the castle of Vistars, free Opil and the Wizard. But how?

Obviously the only means of terrifying the mass of warriors stationed here was to start playing pranks. The idea of killing them off while I was invisible was totally against my basic nature, though surely I would have done even this in order to save Princess Illa, if this were the only way. But I realized I had a second and more honorable choice. First I wanted to get to Lord Waja. If this officer were terrified enough it would automatically follow that his orders would rid the castle automatically of the total of the Vistar unit.

A few more warriors came down the corridor. I stepped in front of them, said, "Leave the castle of Xalla!"

They all paled, looking at the empty space in front of them.

I pushed the first two men.

They fell to the floor on their backs, loud screams of terror uttering from their lips. Then they were up and running down the hall with their companion who had already retreated.

"Leave the castle!" I shouted after them. "Leave the castle or die. The ghost of Xalla speaks."

Several doors opened and heads looked out into the hallway. I laughed hauntingly and repeated my command.

The doors slammed shut.

I started down the hall and found a stairway. Up in the tower would be the room in which Illa was held. Instinctively I started to move in that direction. No sooner had I taken my first step up the stairs than the sound of running footsteps came from behind me.

Some ten warriors rushed into the hall from which I had just stepped. Danj was in charge.

"Now," he announced, "you will find whatever is in here and dispose of it!"

All faces were grim, white, as they drew their weapons and started searching the empty air surrounding them.

I repressed a chuckle and started up the stairs. I determined to question the very next man I passed. I had almost reached the top stair when a warrior came down in my direction.

I grabbed his harness as he started past. He gasped in surprised terror as I lifted him from behind.

"Where will the ghost of Xalla find Lord Waja? Tell me or death will be yours!" I shook him like a dog might a rat. "Speak, fast!"

"Don't kill me...don't kill me!" he fairly screamed in a high-pitched trembling voice.

"Lord Waja!"

116

"In the tower...the tower, the prisoners. With the prisoners!" the man babbled. "Word came that we are...to kill Xalla and his...woman...girl...and—"

I released the poor fellow and he fell down several stairs before regaining his balance enough to half stumble the rest of the way to the lower floor.

I continued, now determined to be done with Waja.

The sound of confusion reigned from below as the warrior I had questioned joined the others. I hurried up one flight of stairs and then another. Now I began taking the steps three at a time, holding to the sword-sheath so that it would not clatter. The thought of what Lord Waja might be up to right at that moment was enough to send chills down my spine.

I passed several warriors on my way up but this time I remained silent, frozen against the wall as they went by.

I kept running up one flight of stairs after another— seemingly an endless series of staircases. Then finally I came to the top of the last flight and found myself facing a long hall. To my right at the end of the corridor stood two guards in front of a door.

I heard a scream. Then another.

I approached the two warriors, momentarily forgetting my invisibility.

The two men turned at my footsteps. Their faces blanched.

"What was that?" one said.

The other shook his head from side to side, then reached for his long sword.

"Where is Lord Waja!" I demanded when but a few heads from the pair of now frightened warriors.

One gasped, stiffened, stifled a scream. He whipped out his sword.

"Speak!" I cried, "or the ghost of Xalla will strike!" I drew my own sword, engaged the warrior who held his weapon, without making an effort to kill or wound.

The effect was as fully rewarding as if I *had* attempted to run the man through.

The unmistakable ring of metal on metal, the movement of his sword as mine pushed it aside was more than either of them could take.

He screamed, dropped his weapon and ran down the hall. The other stood there, white, trembling.

"Go! Before I kill you!" I warned, touching the man's chest with the point of my sword.

He ran after the other Vistar, stumbling down the staircase like a man possessed with total madness.

I reached for the door, attempted to open it. It was locked from the inside. Frantically I began hammering against it with my shoulder, but it would not give even to my greatest efforts.

A voice cried out from beyond it.

"Who is that? Go away or I'll have you killed!" It was Lord Waja, his voice thick with emotion.

I was already beginning to examine the hallway to see if there might be a panel which would take me into a secret passageway, and then into the room.

My hands began to run along the wall, searching for some panel which might open to my touch as had all the others. It seemed to take forever and my mind was frantic with a wild picture of what was surely going on in the room with Lord Waja and the helpless woman. I heard screams which I could now recognize as Illa's.

Time was working against me.

Suddenly my hands felt the wall give. Immediately a panel opened. I slipped into the secret corridor and fairly rushed along the wall. Another panel opened, only to reveal an empty cell. I heard one piercing scream. Then the sound of a large form hitting against something solid. A man's laughter followed.

Frantically I searched for another panel; my fingers found it. A moment later I leaped into the room beyond.

A large bed was centered at the far wall. Lord Waja was leaning over the half conscious form of Illa. The clothing had been all but torn from her lovely body.

With a curse I rushed forward, yanked Lord Waja by the shoulders, throwing him halfway across the room to smack against the wall.

118

He screamed, turned, looked in all directions for his attacker, then sank against the wall, sliding to the floor.

I laughed a forced, angry laugh. "You die!" I screamed, drawing my weapon. "The Ghost of Xalla seeks his revenge!"

As I stepped forward and stopped in front of the half sitting, half lying man, the desire for cold-blooded murder suddenly drained from me. How could I kill such a helpless victim? Then I remembered what he had been trying to do to Illa. My sword touched his chest.

He screamed, his face crumbled, and suddenly he froze like an ice image of a man; those weak features set hard, chalk-white, terror marked itself on each line.

I leaned down, examined the man, and immediately realized he was dead.

Turning, I gazed upon Illa, my heart pounding with excitement and love, relief and so much emotion that it was all but impossible to control myself. She was alive, safe—at least for the moment.

She lay there in the bed staring at Lord Waja, wide-eyed, her face devoid of color.

Suddenly I realized what was frightening her.

"Illa, it's I!" my voice exclaimed, as I thought hard to bring visibility back. "I, Thoris of Rota."

She gasped, her eyes suddenly focusing upon the area in which I stood.

Then a cry of warning broke from her lips.

"So," came a cold voice from the direction of the panel in which I had entered the room. "It is you—not a ghost!"

I turned to see Danj, blade in hand, stepping into the room.

Chapter Eleven

Draught of Invisibility

"Where did you come from?" I blurted in surprise. He was the last person I expected to see here, stepping out of the secret passageway.

"I followed the reports of the 'Ghost'. The hall panel into this secret passageway was open. I investigated. Not all Vistars believe in ghosts!" Danj announced sarcastically.

"You have demoralized our whole unit, warrior. But once they find that the great ghost of Xalla is but a mere cowardly warrior—and see his dead body—they will quickly recover!" He snarled as he moved from the panel to the center of the room with the grace of a dancer. "Now we will truly see who is the best swordsman!"

I dashed to the panel, kicked it shut. It pushed back into place, revealing not even a hair line seam to indicate that it ever existed.

"The pleasure is mine," I said, turning to the Vistar swordsman. "Now things are even!"

The two of us faced each other, swords extended but not touching. We circled around like two wary cats, carefully sizing up the other before embracing in a life and death struggle.

Then I touched his blade, the ringing sound clashing against the room's walls. "Come!"

Danj's sword instantly weaved through a series of feints, lunges, swings, so rapidly that it took all my efforts to keep from being run through.

120

I heard a gasp of fear escape Illa, and out of the corner of my eye I saw her sitting up in the bed, right hand covering her mouth.

"Princess...there is nothing to worry about...this kloof could not kill me if my back was turned...Not if his life depended on it—and it does!" I gasped between defensive movements to keep away from the naked point of Danj's sword. My words were more for Danj than Illa. Long experience had taught me that the best way to put a swordsman off balance was to get him emotionally upset.

Danj cursed and redoubled his efforts to be done with me. I parried each attack, remaining on the defensive.

Sweat broke out over Danj's forehead and body as he moved the sword from one attack to another, carving a deadly screen of steel before him which would have quickly bettered most expert swordsmen. The effective moves of my own weapon to ward off death were having a strong influence on the man. He had not expected my survival for much longer than the first few moments of the duel. And surely if any of his attacks had connected I would have been dead, instantly.

"You fight hard," he admitted at the extreme point of a lunge. "But you will die nonetheless." Our blades locked at that moment. For some time the two of us strained against one another, then I leaped back.

"Not yet, Vistar." I had backed away from another lunge and now took the offensive, swinging at his head with a feint, then bringing my sword down, low toward his stomach and then up around at the chest. He let me play out each feint and met my sword at the point where the true attack was aimed.

"Cute, but primitive!" he mocked, his lips twisting into a crooked sneer. But the eyes revealed a flicker of fear.

Now his sword was moving in quick little actions to meet each attack. All the time his thin lips grinned tauntingly across those crooked teeth.

I had met many swordsmen in my own country but none with Danj's grace. We continued back and forth, taking turns playing the defensive and offensive roles, changing parts like the players of some fantastically childish game.

The ring of steel was deafening in the close confines of the room.

Then suddenly I felt the prick of steel cut across my chest.

"You tire," he suggested in a taunting voice as he attempted to repeat his success.

But this time I countered with a double feint to his head, just as he was attempting to back me against the bed. I followed this with an attack and feint at the chest, then a cross-cut to the stomach. My blade nicked the soft flesh of his right side.

He backed away, startled. The grin froze.

I doubled my efforts, now attempting to keep him on the defensive. And again my blade drank blood, cutting downwards. He cursed, lunged and lunged again. I parried each attack, and then cut under his guard to touch his right arm.

"You weaken, Vistar," I taunted. Now he was on the run, a position which a man like Danj disliked with a vengeance, for swordsman though he was, his heart was cowardly. And like all men, he did not want to die. Each touch had thrown him off just a little bit more. He was beginning to show signs of mental breakdown, panic. His eyes blinked more quickly, his lips compressed, jerking ever so slightly. He attacked, his blade flashing before him, cutting at my guard like a madman, again attempting to back me into the bed where he might throw my body off balance enough to make the kill. But instead of backing up, I stood my ground and after a moment returned his attack with one of my own.

"Now, I think I'll kill you, Vistar!" I lunged into a complicated series of feints and cuts which touched him three times.

He was sweating furiously; blood mixed with sweat to run down his body in long red streaks. The look in his eyes was wild, animal, without a natural calmness of humanity. The fear of death was breathing down his back, absorbing into his muscles like poison.

Frantically he swung at my head, then came back for my stomach. I felt the sting of the sword just touch my flesh but apparently no blood had been drawn for he did not seem to notice. Nevertheless his attack renewed with maddening intensity—as if reason and logic had left his mind, as if pure fury had taken control of all muscles, melting skill and coolness away as heat will melt the fat of an animal. I'm sure he was near the point of total insanity for he moved with such renewed strength that it could have been caused only by such a mental breakdown.

I met each attack with an ease which even surprised myself. It surely seemed to have shocked Danj. There was now a total sense of calm flowing over my nerves and muscles. The end was near and both of us knew it. I kept my eyes on the other's movements and countered them with quick defensive actions of my own.

He was now breathing quite heavily and the pressure of his sword against mine was considerably lessened. I let him continue to play out his waning strength. Then when he leaped forward in an awkward lunge, I easily pushed his sword aside and touched him twice on the chest in a deep crisscross cut.

Now I took complete control of the duel. I was able to touch him almost at any moment, though unable to bring it to an end, for his guard was still quick enough to elude death.

Danj was covered from head to waist with a series of bloody cuts. His face etched deep with raw, naked terror now, for he knew that death was near.

Finally Danj backed up against a corner. I feinted again at his chest, then lunged. His guard and reactions had weakened, slowed, and this time his blade was not where it should have been. I felt the point of my weapon push into and enter his chest. The blade sank completely through flesh and bone and stopped against the hard stone wall at his back.

Danj stood there, sword still clasped in his hand, an expression of total shock marring his features. He started to say something but no sound came. Blood trickled from his thin mouth. Then slowly his muscles relaxed. A moment later he was dead. I let my sword fall with his body.

Turning, I looked at Illa. She fairly leaped to her feet, ran into my arms, sobbing like a little child. "I thought...you would be killed..."

Words burst from my lips before I realized what I had said. Some burning need within me, some wild, overwhelming passion controlled my voice.

"I love you, Princes Illa." There was no mistaking my total meaning, my hot, fiery passion which made those words fraught with emotion.

Slowly she stiffened and then pushed away. "You cannot love your Princess! Not in that way!"

She turned then, presenting her back to me. I thought I heard a soft sob, then after a brief moment she said: "We must get out of this horrible place. But how?" As she now faced me, her features were puzzled and frightened.

For the first time I remembered how bad our position was. The Vistars were still in control of the castle. I was visible. It would be necessary to return to the Chambers of Wizardry on order to regain invisibility. Once the Vistars knew that their leader was dead, and Danj, their greatest swordsman, defeated, they would surely believe they had no chance to survive long in Xalla's castle.

"Where's Opil kept?" I asked.

Illa's face tightened just a little with a hard emotion, then relaxed slightly. "In the cell next to mine. There!" She pointed to the right.

"We'll get her out and then try to find the Chambers of Wizardry through the secret passageway."

I pulled Illa after me, moving to the door, which we opened and I carefully looked into the corridor beyond. I had picked Danj's fallen sword from the floor next to his body as I passed, and now held it ready for any emergency. But there was no one in the hallway.

I went to the door behind which Opil was supposed to be confined, and attempted to open it. To my pleasure it came easily unlatched.

Illa explained, "They open from the outside, unless locked from within by a special key. Complicated, but useful. Such locks are in the Wizard's Place in Muda."

No sooner had I opened the door to Opil's room than the woman cried out in sudden joy and came running across to me, throwing her arms around my neck. I was so stunned

124

and embarrassed that it was quite impossible to do anything other than stand there, shocked.

"Oh, Thoris," Opil fairly cried in pleasure, "you are alive, free! Oh, blessed be my father for saving you!"

She released me and then looked up into my eyes like an adoring child. "What now, Thoris the Mighty?"

"Do you know the way along the secret passages to the Chamber of Wizardry?" I inquired without any preamble.

She frowned as if she didn't understand what I was talking about.

I quickly explained what had happened between her father and myself, and then she shook her head. "I know nothing of a secret passageway. But if we can get to the Chambers of Wizardry, I can mix potions which will defeat the Vistar flegs!"

"Invisibility is enough!" I pointed out.

I now led the two women out into the corridor and then we entered the secret passageway, closing the panel behind us.

Opil and Illa clung close to me as we moved along the passageway. Finally we came to stairs leading downwards, and began the long descent in our search for the Chambers of Wizardry. I noticed that each time we came to a floor, Opil counted half to herself and finally, after sometime, she softly said: "It should be here on this level!"

We had gone down some twenty floors.

I quickly surveyed the corridor and in a moment saw that Opil had been correct, for just ten heads away a dozen dead bodies lay before one of the panels.

We made our way to this point and I pushed the bodies aside so that the women didn't have to step over them. A moment later we were in the Chambers of Wizardry.

I started for the bench which held the bottles of liquid that had been mixed under the directions of the Wizard of Zorkada. Opil was immediately at my side. She understood the meaning of the bottles and at once combined them in a large beaker.

"We'll all become invisible!" she suggested.

I started to object but Illa quickly agreed. Opil took several large swallows of the invisibility liquid and passed it over to Illa, who without hesitation followed her example. All this happened too fast for me to interfere.

As Illa passed the beaker to me, Opil began flickering, then her image abruptly flashed out of existence. Illa gasped, then Opil laughed.

"It works fast!" she giggled, delighted.

As I finished off the beaker, Illa too disappeared from sight.

A moment later the two girls said that I had vanished too.

"Now what?" Illa inquired, breathlessly, like a little child about to start on an exciting game.

Opil answered: "Take care of the Vistars!"

"Let's not go off half-armed!" I quickly outlined to them a plan that I thought was the quickest way of ridding the castle of the Vistars, ending with: "I don't want either of you taking any unnecessary chances. Make your statements at a safe distance, and move quickly away!"

Opil asked: "What about father?"

I had forgotten the Wizard's last statement to me before he finally vanished. "I'd better free him—or at least get some medicine to him at once! He was weak from exhaustion and lack of food and water. He said something about his Inner Resources disappearing."

A gasp sucked from Opil's lips. She sounded more frightened than I had ever heard a person sound before. "We must move fast!"

Suddenly a bottle disappeared from the bench in front of us. "This will revive him! If it isn't too late!" she cried. "The liquid has all the food value and power to make him totally new. He will regain the strength of a giant. I'll go to him immediately."

I started to object, then decided this was probably the best thing Opil could do. There was little danger, and possibly if the Wizard would gain entrance to the Chambers of Wizardry, we would have lessened our problem with the Vistars. I told Opil where to look.

After she had left I automatically motioned Illa to my side, then remembered that she could not see me.

"Illa, into the secret passage. We'll stay together, get to the outside corridor and..."

I heard a scream of terror from beyond the walls of the room and guessed it was because Opil had whispered ghostly threats of death and decay to some helpless warriors, as I had instructed her.

In moments Illa and myself were in the corridor outside the Chamber of Wizardry on our way to the throne room. There we found half a dozen warriors and officers, all talking in harsh terror of the reports of the ghost of Xalla.

I said loud enough for all to hear: "Lord Waja is dead—and you will find him in the cell where you kept the women prisoners. Danj has fallen before the blade of Xalla's ghost! And such will be the fate of all who stay!"

I immediately moved to another location after finishing my statement. Then Illa's voice sighed mistily from the throne as if blown from the throat of some Wind Goddess: "Leave the Castle of Xalla—or die! The castle warns you!"

I was holding my sword in my hand, and with this I gently poked one of the stiffened Vistar officers, touching his back with the lightness of air.

He screamed as if mortally stabbed, leaped around to face his attacker as if burned with the fires.

"I, Xalla, strike!" my voice rang out menacingly upon the deathly silence of the room. "Die!"

The officer became a tortured mad animal, fleeing for the exit. I don't think he stopped until he had reached the courtyard. The others watched with wide-eyed fascination, terror rippling through the air from one to the other. Then as I laughed malevolently they stared in the direction of my voice, dumb creatures, mindless, for such was the power of fear over them that they were not quite human—reason was slipping from their reality.

Illa blew windy threats from the throne: "Go, before you all die. Xalla will strike you dead as he struck Lord Waja, without a blow!"

With that they shrank from the throne room like cowering shadows, voiceless in terror to make their way toward the courtyard where wild, excited voices now fairly screamed orders.

127

I called to Illa, and the two of us silently followed. Now we listened. It was obvious that one of the officers who had not been in the throne room had taken charge, saying "He is dead. Not a scratch. Like the voice said. Danj is cut to ribbons—dead!"

A rumbling murmur raced around the courtyard in which all the Vistars had now assembled.

The officer's voice bellowed: "A ghost cannot kill. This is not possible! We will seek out that which is causing this and—"

Suddenly his voice cut off as if cut in two. In front of him appeared such a sight that my own throat constricted with shocked surprise.

Multi-colored smoke billowed up from the air itself, greens, blues and reds flashed, sparks flared, showering those around like a fountain of light, then a giant form slowly took shadowy shape, growing larger and larger, looming above the Vistars. The form was robed, a long white beard hung from its face. Arms rose high towards the sky once it had attained a height of twenty heads, a loud maniacal laugh reverberated throughout the courtyard. Those giant arms fell downwards like long thick whips, sparks of lightning flashing from the gnarled fingers, directly towards the man in front of him.

The officer of the Vistar suddenly went rigid; his body swelled as if it were filling with water; the shell of flesh and muscle strained like a balloon under too much pressure, then exploded. A moment later there was nothing other than a few shreds of skin and shards of bloody bone to indicate that he had ever existed.

"Leave!" came the cackling voice of Xalla, Wizard of Zorkada.

He turned, his hands tracing along the ground at the feet of the of the Vistar warriors. Fire crackled at the Vistar feet, burning flame that ate all it touched.

In but a moment the other Vistars had fled, rushing in panic for the closed gate beyond which was the escape of a moat, meadow and a forest. The gate raised automatically as if some ghostly hand had moved it, and the yellow-clad warriors dashed out of the Castle of Xalla. None looked back.

When the last if the Vistars had disappeared into the forest, the tall gate closed and the giant image of the Wizard abruptly vanished. A few moments later Opil and a gnarled old man stepped into the courtyard.

"Thoris, where are you?" Opil cried, looking from left to right around the court.

I had been far too taken aback by what had just happened to remember that the invisibility potion was still in effect. Now I willed myself back to normal. A moment later, after telling Illa how to regain visibility, I saw her appear at my side. It was all I could do to keep from pulling her into my arms, covering her face with kisses. Then my attention was drawn fully to Opil.

The daughter of the Wizard of Zorkada rushed into my arms, sobbing like a little child. Then I heard a startling and unnerving statement from her lips: "I love you, Thoris the Mighty! Oh, I love you!"

Gently, but firmly, I moved the woman from me. "You don't know what you are saying."

She violently shook her head. "I have loved you from the beginning. I have loved you since I saw you fighting so magnificently in the forest for the honor and life of Opil, Daughter of Xalla, Wizard of Zorkada! Fighting for me while not even knowing for whom you fought. I decided then that you would be mine. I realized then that the legend was true. You will marry me, Thoris the Mighty, and become a student of my father, and have all the riches and honors which are the station of the Son of Xalla and husband of his daughter! Thus it has been written long before I was born."

I stood there like a man of stone. Words would not form, for what words could honestly express my true feelings without mortally hurting this young girl? There was no doubt in my mind that I wanted nothing to do with her offer, regardless of the fact that Opil was a most attractive woman. Also there was no doubt that Opil was serious. The determined look in her eyes held no room for arguments. She expected me to embrace her and state my undying love. I dreaded to think what she might do if I now spoke the truth.

That she could love me seemed fantastic. But then, had I not fallen totally in love with Illa, Princess of Haldolen, at first sight? Could not another fall in love in such a manner? Even with a common warrior as myself?

At that point Xalla stepped forward and looked at my face. He was far smaller than his mental projection had been, not topping my chest. His face crinkled into a maze of lines. There was a sharp fire of wisdom in his aged eyes.

"We meet for the first time, Thoris. And I have promised what I have promised: Safe passage through the lands of Zorkada and a safe means to reach the land of your choice, no matter where they might be!" Then he winked. "But this hardly is enough for what you have done for my people and my daughter and for the Wizard of Zorkada! For word had come to Waja that Zorkada's defeat was total. He was to kill Opil and myself. What manner of reward could an old man offer to repay such a debt? But Opil, my beautiful daughter, has found one reward greater than you requested, which is, again, but a token payment for all that you have done for my people. It is up to you to decide, and I would suggest that you stay here for a few days before making any such decision. It is far better to wait and carefully think over such a serious decision." He winked again.

He was a wise old man; and I could see a bright twinkle in his eyes. But what the twinkle and wink might denote was impossible to guess.

The outcome was that I give Opil no answer at this time, and that we have a banquet, and feast upon the foods of Zorkada and the wines of Xalla.

"We will free those servants who are in the dungeons below and they will prepare a feast such as you have never experienced," Xalla announced. Then he reached for Illa, who hesitated, obviously frightened.

He said: "You will come with me and I will be honored to show you some quarters. Fear not, young woman, for Xalla with all his magical powers could not for the life of him restore his body to youth. Opil will see to Thoris the Mighty after which we will free our servants and prepare a feast!"

CHAPTER TWELVE

HELL HATH NO FURY...

I stood there in the courtyard, uneasy, aware of the trap in which Xalla had placed me. I did not doubt he would be quick to anger if the proper cause presented itself, and I did not look forward to turning down his daughter as a wife and mate.

Opil took my arm and there was something about the way her fingers held me which indicated far too well the difficulty I was about to face.

She said gaily: "You have done so much for which Xalla and I will be eternally grateful. You are truly Mighty. And a woman of my station would not offer herself to a mere common warrior. I must mate only with the greatest of all warriors, and I have known none so great as you, Thoris."

As Opil spoke she was guiding me across the courtyard to one of the stairways which led up toward the many apartments.

"I have not made my offer lightly, Thoris. I will mate with none other than you. It is my wish that you fully understand that. I want you to know that I will have my way—I *will* have you!" She said this so casually, but with such a tone of conviction in her voice, that my spine became a stalactite.

If only Illa, Princess of Haldolen, could be as open and free with her affections as this daughter of a Wizard was to me! If only Illa were not a Princess and could love me, a common warrior of Haldolen.

Finally we came to a small doorway which Opil opened to present a large beautifully furnished apartment.

"This is where you will stay." Opil was now very close to me and I could smell the sweet perfume of her body. She looked up into my eyes, head slightly upturned so that her lovely lips were but a short distance from mine. "Thoris, you must learn the true passion of this woman who would have you for her lover, her warrior, her husband, Lord and mate!"

All at once her arms encircled my neck. She pressed her body to mine. I felt the trembling hot kisses of her lips cover my mouth. It took some moments to disengage myself from that embrace.

"Opil!" I scolded, amazed by this woman's brash boldness. No woman of Haldolen would act thus. "Don't make things harder than they are!"

Her face contorted, and for a moment I felt the full fury of her intense dark eyes. There was some uncanny, unfathomable power in her furious gaze. I felt an odd helplessness, almost an emotional wave of pleasure soothe over my nerves.

Then Opil once more attempted to come into my arms.

I thought of Illa, of that beautiful, proud woman who had held all my true love and filled my every thought since the first moment we met on the galley *Vayis,* so short a time before. A woman who would surely never allow me to some so close to her. Then realizing my true feelings, I pushed Opil gently away—freed of the sudden mystical spell her gaze had cast over me. I had a firm grip on her shoulders, and it was with an effort I kept from shaking her, such was my own sudden fury.

"This can never be for you, Opil. I cannot be yours for my heart is already held by another."

"It's that slave! She'll be dead before the sun moves one degree in the sky!"

I gripped Opil harder, hurting her and not caring. "If you harm her, I'll kill you, Opil. That's a promise."

There was a tense violence in my voice which seemed to have struck Opil. She shook her head slowly; the rage slackened from her oval face.

"Thoris, think carefully about what I offer. Think *very* carefully, for fatal danger lies beyond refusal of my love. I would rather see you dead than in the arms of another. I have promised what I promised! I know the strain of this day has hampered your thinking. But think hard, warrior— for you walk among the shadows of death!" With that she stomped from the room.

As I stood there watching until she disappeared down the stairway, I felt a cold shivery presentiment of evil. There was so much raw violence in Opil that I now feared for the safety of my Princess. What secrets of Wizardry did she know? What magic could she summon to power which might bring danger to myself or Illa? My sword could surely sink into her flesh and drink her blood; and I would rather do such than have her take the life of the Princess of Haldolen.

After a moment I examined my surroundings to discover myself assigned to a luxurious room with a large bed, big enough to sleep three, curtained in red drapes of shiny cloth. A wall rack for weapons was on the far side of the bed, holding a delicately jeweled harness and a long sword.

The bed attracted me, for it was soft, comfortable, deeply padded.

It was then that I realized that exhaustion had finally taken its toll of my strength.

I fell to the bed and the next thing I was aware of was the sound of insistent pounding on the door.

I sat up, dazed from the dream which had haunted my sleep. A dream which slipped from memory almost immediately.

Standing, I went to the door and opened it. A tall handsome man stood there in jeweled warrior harness.

"I am to inform you that Opil, Beautiful Daughter of Exalted Wizard of Zorkada, and her Wondrous Father, Xalla, are waiting you in the banquet halls. You are requested to change into the clothing which is in this room."

"I will be with you directly." I turned and examined the harness on the wall next to the bed. It was that of a noble of high rank. In moments I had stripped out of the plain harness of common warrior and slipped into the jeweled trappings. Then I joined the man and followed him down to the courtyard below.

My mind was trying to remember the elusive dream which had plagued my sleep. It had something to do with Opil, but memory was receding through the thick fog.

Once in the courtyard we proceeded to the corridor which led to the throne room. My eyes paused on the huge dragon-like snake of gold set in the doorway of the outer entrance and a chill iced my vertebrae. This carving aroused some distant memory which seemed to have something to do with my dream. Those bulging evil eyes looked down with horrid intent. I could almost feel that mouth breathing at me, that forked tongue lancing out at my face, those large carved fangs snapping hungrily. The detail was so startlingly lifelike that it was not difficult to imagine that it could spring into animation.

I said to the man: "That's a marvelous carving, who molded it?"

"The Dragon of Xalla?" He turned to me. "They say it was alive, that it is an enchanted dragon and that Xalla, with his magic, can bring it back to life to threaten those who would threaten this castle."

"I wonder, then, why he didn't do so today, using the dragon against the Vistars?"

"I have heard that even Xalla might not be able to control it. Great magic was used to encase it in the doorway."

"When was this done?"

"A hundred, three-hundred Four-Seasons ago."

"But surely Xalla could not have—"

"They say that the wizard has lived a thousand Four-Seasons. I do not know. But as long as I have lived he has been as he is today. Who knows what magic our beloved Wizard might have to give eternal life?"

We had come now to the double door which led to the throne. It automatically opened at our approach.

The sight which met my eyes was totally different from that which I had expected. The throne room had been transformed into a huge feasting hall with a long transparent table in its center, heavy laden with platters of food, whole sides of beef, lamb, hog, huge game birds, surrounded with roasted fruits, goblets of many different wines, colored from white and pink to deep purple-reds, exotic looking vegetables—enough food to feed a hundred starving warriors. Surely more than four people could eat in a Season.

To my left four men stood in the corner of the room, holding unusual string instruments upon which they played a weird but pleasant melody. Dancing girls in filmy gowns swayed to its rhythm on the far side of the room. Sitting on the throne was Xalla. A silvery robe flickering with distant stars flowed over his small gnarled body. On a golden pillow sat Illa, and on his left was Opil, who rose and quickly glided across the room and took my arm in a boldly possessive manner.

"You are rested, my Thoris?" she inquired, pulling me to the throne.

"I rested well." I felt a sense of annoyance and uneasiness. My glance went to Illa and within me a longing cried to be at her side. She hardly seemed to notice my entrance.

"You did not dream?" Opil questioned casually.

I frowned, puzzled by this question, for it seemed so out of context.

"It is enough that you slept. One must rest and be rested and become new again. That is all that matters. I hope that your sleep was dreamless." But there was that about her voice which indicated something quite different than her words suggested.

Xalla rose from the throne and stepped down to my side. "You are a true hero of our people. I have notified our great leader, Hallis, Ruler of Zorkada, and he sends his greetings and offers you a Lordship in his Kingdom if you will but stay on and make this your home." He glanced at Opil at my side as if to say, "and my daughter as your woman."

"You and your Ruler are far too generous. I only did what was necessary and could not have done anything but for your help, most powerful Wizard."

135

He chuckled at that, then clapped his hands. "We begin. Sit beside me, there!" He indicated the left of the throne next to which were two purple pillows.

Opil fairly dragged me forward. Illa sat rigidly as I approached. She was draped in a golden gown which flowed over her beautiful body like the waves of sunlight caressing the ocean.

A moment later I found myself studying Opil, noticing her black gown, and thinking how much that color fit her, for she was as black as night, mysterious. As with the night, the real Opil seemed to be hidden in the shadows. One could sense unspeakable powers in the gloomy dark, like invisible demons, waiting to be called up.

I wondered why it was that I could feel nothing for Opil. Maybe because of this suggestion of evil which lurked in the subdued lighting of her features. Yet this woman was offering me a position which did not seem possible under any other circumstances, and certainly not in Haldolen: Riches, wisdom, and, if the servant I had talked to before entering the room a little while ago was right about the agelessness of Xalla, endless life. What else could a common warrior desire?

Opil winked. "I think you will enjoy yourself tonight. The entertainment is the finest we have in all Zorkada. But don't enjoy yourself *too* much!" Her eyes flashed toward the dancers.

She directed my attention to these swaying dancers who had now slipped up to the open space in front of the throne. The lovely young girls moved gracefully to the unfamiliar sounds of the three stringed instruments. There was an exotic beauty about their movements, the way the gowns moved around their bodies, the way their legs moved from one step to another as if gliding on frozen water.

I asked where the girls had come from and Opil answered: "From Zorkada. Our Ruler sent them to entertain the guests of Xalla. They came by balloon, of course!" This revealed little to me and I had no chance to inquire further since at that moment a servant offered me a large goblet which contained a clear amber liquid. Opil took the other goblet from the golden tray as the man held it out to her.

I looked toward Illa and found her staring at me; there was an odd flashing fire in her eyes, a red flush hot on her cheeks. She hurriedly turned away, looked up at the Wizard, as if deeply engrossed in what the old man was saying.

"This liquid is of the Gods," Opil said, as my attention returned to her. "Xalla and his great genius can bring magic to all liquids."

Xalla explained: "I call it Zor-Ka. All of our lands pay high prices for this brew which the Castle of Xalla furnishes to the markets and shops of Zorkada."

"We make much more income in such a manner," Opil pointed out. "That and the spells which my glorious father can cast. He sells everything from charms for luck to potions for love. His magic is thus given for the whole of Zorkada. But such forms of simple tricks and potions are almost annoying to my father—he could use someone like you to perform these for the city-folk, leaving him more time to devote to studies of the Secrets of the Universe. Still how is one to survive without such means of support? The government of Zorkada pays high for his protection yet it is not enough for him to live in the style to which he has become used."

"Enough conversation," Xalla admonished. "Drink, be happy. Enjoy the feast!"

I sipped the amber drink and found its taste much like honey, though hardly as sweet. There were scented undertones to the flavor that I could not place. A soft soothing glow flowed over my body and immediately I felt relaxed and at ease with the world. I sipped some more and discovered that the liquid was marvelous in flavor, which now detailed all its subtle seasonings to my abruptly alert tastes. Again I sipped and the world seemed to brighten, burst alive, my senses fairly swelling outwards to embrace everything within sight.

For a moment this seemed to be the same potion which the Wizard had had me take the day I first fought Danj. But after sometime I realized there was a total difference in this Zor-Ka brew.

I turned to face Opil. I had almost an irresistible impulse to look at her, as if drawn by some magnetic mystical force.

Her dark eyes seemed like transparent pools of night in which I could see the bottomless deeps of her soul. It was a beautiful, lovely soul. The gentle, caressing perfections of Womanhood, willing to give so much, willing to submit to all desire. She leaned close and touched my cheek with her fingertips and I felt dangerous desire pulse in my veins. The sudden urge to embrace her was all but overwhelming; it enveloped me like some invisible fog, some alien will.

I shook my head, then sipped more of the Zor-Ka. I found myself studying the dancing girls. All at once I wanted to embrace each of those slender young forms. It was a strange and even frightening experience.

I sipped more liquid and felt myself slipping into a deep invisible whirling waterless pool. The sensations of that evening are beyond my ability to fully describe.

Platters of food came in the hands of servants and we feasted until it was impossible to eat more. Then upon quaffing the liquid of the Gods, the fullness seemed to vanish. Again and again we feasted upon each platter of food, gorging ourselves on the rare meats, the steaming vegetables and cooled fruits until it was again impossible to eat more. Then again our goblets would be filled and we drank. Hunger surged through me and again it was satisfied by limitless portions of delicious food.

Time seemed to waver, to take on vague flow which blurred out of detail. Actions blended into other actions. I drank, then ate, then drank again, only to fill the craving of my newly born hunger with more food.

I remember once looking around the room, studying the walls, and becoming almost hypnotized by two beautifully silvery spears, whose shafts were intricately carved by some artist whose skill was surely of the highest in the world.

It was a dizzy madness and through the conversation and laughter I discovered that not once did I think of Illa but instead found my attention and total desires focusing feverishly on Opil, this fascination of Womanhood who was so yielding, so willing to share herself with the warrior whom she loved. Countless times her hands would reach for me, caressingly.

How long this continued I have no idea. Time had passed, evening into night and night into early morning. The dancers kept dancing without stop, the food continued to be brought forward, the goblets always seemed full. Then finally Opil moved gracefully to her feet and reached down for me. I rose beside her, trembling from the erotic excitement which her inviting smile aroused in me. I moved like a mothka drawn toward a candle's burning wick, holding her hand. All thoughts centered on the promise of her smile, the flow and rhythm of her form as it glided gracefully across the throne room and out into the corridor, then beyond to the courtyard, upon which flooded soft golden glows from the face of Lonu the Moon.

"My father," Opil murmured, her face close to mine, "has said that the moon is a world like the one we now inhabit. But I do not understand. I believe that our world is floating upon an endless sea. Scientists have different theories about our world and the moon. All I know is that the moon, for us and young Zorkadians who think not about the details of science, is the Goddess of Love. She has always shone for lovers. And I imagine it will be so throughout the ages." Opil was leaning close and I could smell the scented oils in which her body had been bathed. I was drunk from liquor and food, yet in total control of my muscles; it was not the drunkenness of liquor as served in the Bots Area of Muda but an amazingly different kind of inebriation—as if I were detached, another person, unrelated to the one I was when normally sober.

I could look at Opil and feel all the urges which such a beautiful woman will inspire in man; the desire to protect, to hold, to be with through eternity. It was a sublime sublunar magic there in the courtyard of Xalla's castle—but at the same time an unholy kind of magic for it was evoked by the liquids of the Gods, Zor-Ka, a tainted spell created solely for the purpose of clouding one's reason and producing a false romantic madness.

When I reached for Opil to pull her into my arms, I thought nothing of the right or wrong of it. It seemed natural and very normal. After all, I was in love, and this woman was in love with me. The fact that I loved only Illa, Princess of Haldolen, had nothing to do with my reasoning. Opil was Womanhood and, being such, was all women, or *the* Woman, the ideal perfection upon which all mortal man could shower his passion and love.

Strangely enough, as I reached for Opil, she slipped away.

"Not here," she whispered. "In your room. Then we will fulfill the divine rightness of our first meeting in the forest, when you saved me from the Vistar warriors. You will know that we were created by the Gods for one another. There we will learn the total frankness of what we are, of what we can be and what we will be to each other for eternity.

"For it is written that a tall warrior and maid would someday come into my life, when such a warrior was needed most, and that he would be the man of my heart! It is written that he would save us all, that he would be worshiped by our people! And you are that warrior, Thoris the Mighty! And because of that I fell in love with you that first day, that very first moment that I set eyes upon your strong young form. What a wonderful sight it is to see you fighting against an enemy. Your sword flashing surely in and out, weaving such a net of wizardry that no one can long survive its attack!"

I looked at her and realized this was not some mystical Goddess, a perfection of Womanhood, but rather an alien form, a single female, named Opil, daughter of the Wizard of Zorkada. She was not the woman I loved. What spell had she cast to capture my reason for even this long?

I wanted nothing to do with her, now or ever.

The liquor and food had numbed my reason but now, faced with stark reality, the hotness and promise of this woman's words, I knew that even under the power of an evil spell it was impossible to continue like this.

I moved quickly from Opil. It was a night beautiful beyond all imagination to conjure up. The walls of the castle were dark shadows against the soft crystal sky of black which was pinpointed with the flickering fires of the Gods as they warmed the heavens against the cold of night. It was truly a night for lovers, to take the woman into your arms and stroll down a pathway among the flowers of a Goddess Temple. But it was not Haldolen. And I suddenly longed for the cool nights of Haldolen, of the Temple of the Goddess of Rota, where rhozes flanked rock pathways, where one could gaze upon the golden face of the Temple Virgins with its high pillars, upon which stood the gracefully carved figures of lesser goddesses. I longed to hear the soft murmuring of the Virgins' voices as they lifted in the night in worship of our Goddess of Rota, singing Her praises and blessing Her with a long life of eternal happiness, so that she would in turn bless our lands and bring a blooming harvest in both crops and children. I longed for the land of my birth.

I felt Opil at my side. She attempted to take my arm but I drew back.

"What's wrong, Thoris?" she cried.

"This is wrong! All of it. I do not love you, Opil. I wish it were so, for your sake. But the truth is that I do not want you, though you are a most desirable woman, a beautiful woman, as you must surely be aware." I faced her so that the truth of my words would be more strongly apparent, so that she could see with her own eyes that I had been truthful, that I would not weaken ever again. Such love as she wanted was for only those who truly loved. I could feel sorrow for her, for was not my own longing for Illa much the same as hers for me?

"I am sorry, Opil. But I was not meant for you. I am not that warrior of whom you spoke. No doubt another will come. I will be leaving soon and we will never see each other again. *This* is what the Gods have written." My voice was honestly regretful; my words would sting and crush her, and yet this was not my desire. I did not wish to hurt Opil or her father.

With that sudden change of temper, that explosive reversal which will make a storm break instantly upon a calm and peaceful world, Opil became another woman, not soft, not feminine, but hard, cruel. She stared up at me and her face slowly contorted with white hot rage. Hatred incarnate.

"*You* are sorry for *me?* I offer you Opil, not a gutter nymph who would become any man's girl for the moment. I offer the daughter of Xalla! And you feel *sorry* for me!" she screamed. Then her right hand swung out, stinging across my face.

"I'll see that you die before you leave this castle! I'll see you and that Dorba Nymph of Hellis you have as a slave in a hell of madness before the night is passed." She whipped around and dashed into the building.

I was now sober, aware of the real danger which threatened both Illa and myself in the Castle of Xalla the Wizard. I could not chance another day here.

I saw Opil enter a side door under the golden dragon-snake above the outer entrance. Then I passed and hurried to the throne room.

CHAPTER THIRTEEN

REVELATION OF THE WERE-DRAGON

Immediately on my entrance, Xalla stood, raised his hand to the sky. Illa sat beside him, her face harsh, her eyes blazing with a dangerous emotion as they turned to me.

"What happened?" Xalla cried, his voice indicating that he had already guessed.

"Opil. I'm sorry," I said. "It could never work out."

Xalla nodded, but his face was drawn tight, his bushy white eyebrows frowned toward one another to make a crooked pyramid. He looked deeply hurt though resigned and not angered. "I told her that it would not work. The potion which was in your drink would bring out the image of love and convince you that she was the total of all women but it would also bring out the final truth. She was convinced you could not resist her. I am sorry, Thoris, to have been a part of this deception. But it was my hope that you would choose my daughter. You are a mighty warrior and I will never be able to repay you for what you have done for me and my country. And—"

A sudden low but horrible hissing growl sounded from the courtyard. It was so unearthly that all of us turned toward it. The Wizard's words froze hard on his thin lips. My spine became a xylophone made of ice particles.

Then a slurping noise, slimy, sickening, followed. A loud sound like that of a serpent hissing in warning anger, came battering at us.

Xalla gasped. His eyes were wide with horror, his hands trembled as he covered his aged face as if attempting to blot out the abominable sound.

"What is it?" I cried.

"The spell—oh, may the Gods have mercy!" He hurried around the throne and I heard his footsteps as they receded in the distance. His terror was so complete that at first I believed he was attempting to escape, but when his footsteps returned at an even more frantic run I guessed the truth.

"The Chamber's doors are bolted from the inside!" he screamed, still wide-eyed with fear, his whole frail body now trembling convulsively.

Another growling hiss sounded close by, not more than a few heads on the other side of the throne room doors.

Then the huge doors swung open and hot fire snaked out, lashing into the room like spears and arrows, burning whips attempting to beat us.

The huge horrifying head of a golden dragon-snake slid into the room, fire spitting from its nostrils, jaws snapping viscously, forked tongue flicking in and out between the huge curved yellowed fangs. Its body slid like some slippery rope against the floor, looping again into a tight ball next to the entrance. That slimy head moved from side to side, surveying the room, and then finally came to a halt, pointed directly at me and Illa, hateful eyes red with fury.

It was the dragon which hung over the entrance of the castle. The Dragon of Xalla! *The spell had been broken!*

I took a stance in front of the Princess and whipped out the jeweled long-sword at my side.

Xalla screamed: "Kill it—kill it!"

I turned and saw the strangest thing, so unexpected and out of character was it for the aged man. Xalla, the Wizard of Zorkada, stood there at the throne, tears running down his eyes, face haggard, the ancient skin almost pure white.

"Isn't there a way out of here?" I cried.

Xalla shook his head. "The spell—it won't do any good!"

The snake suddenly darted toward me and I recoiled with man's instinctive fear of the reptilian.

As the forked tongue reached greedily out between fangs, my sword swiftly leaped at that black twin-pointed spear of flesh.

144

A scream hissed from the beast's long neck. The dragon retreated; billowing flame burst from its nostrils. There was nothing to do but attack, fast!

I leaped in, attempting to get around behind the head in order to cut at its neck without danger of counterattack.

The snake body coiled before I had covered half the distance. The head jerked forward in swift attack.

Years of training moved the muscles of my arm, the sword lashed out, met the head edge-on, cutting deep into the skull just above the right eye.

What happened immediately after that I don't know, other than suddenly I was whipped around, lifted from the floor. A huge coil of scaly flesh wrapped tightly around me. My sword vainly attempted to cut into the flesh that held my body.

A scream sounded from Princess Illa. Then suddenly I saw a quick movement from Xalla the wizard. He had leaped for one of the long spears on the wall to his right. I was struggling to hold my breath and at the same time attack the coiled tail which was squeezing tighter and tighter in an attempt to crush my body.

The snake head, gigantically proportioned, breathed down at me, closing the gap between us. Nausea attacked my senses.

My sword lunged at the monstrous eyes. The point flicked deep into the soft white pupil of the right eye and then I felt the grip around my body lessen slightly, only to tighten convulsively an instant later.

Black pain scourged through my mind and body, and my lips opened wide to break out with a curse of agony.

Through the black fog I saw the Wizard's robed form leap close; a long silvery spear flung from his hands, then flew toward the frightened serpent head, sinking deep into the lower part of the drooling jaw.

The snake tail released its grip on me and I tumbled to the floor dazed, all but stunned into unconsciousness. Yet my body coiled into immediate action, leaped to its feet, turned, faced the enemy with blade moving almost on its own. My mind was hardly conscious of what my body automatically did.

In battle a warrior either fights with an automatic will, without regard to pain or danger, or he dies in battle as the price for hesitation. I moved close, and the long sword swung, aiming at that thick reptilian neck.

With both hands I swung the sword downward, using every muscle. It was a final, total commitment. If I failed, death would be my reward, for the head was already turned my way, gaping jaws wide, beginning to close.

The sword swung, then connected, true to aim, cutting through the flesh and bone, severing head from body.

I leaped back to escape the convulsive shudders of the death struggle which should follow.

But no sooner had the head fallen than a ghastly crackling sounded through the air and the dragon slowly twisted together, shrinking, curling upon itself, becoming a tight ball! It blurred. A moment later I was looking down upon the headless form of a human being.

For some time I could not believe what had happened. Then slowly, as my gaze moved to where the serpent head had fallen, I felt a shudder of horror. *I saw the lifeless eyes of Opil staring at me,* as if in death gaining one last look at the warrior she had so hopelessly desired.

Illa screamed. Then silence descended on the room.

I felt an ineffable sadness invade my consciousness. I wondered over and over again why Opil should have done such a thing.

Turning, I looked at Illa, then Xalla. My sword moved toward the Wizard for I knew not what to expect.

Xalla was standing in the middle of the room, gazing at the bodiless head of his daughter. For some time he did not move. Tears ran down his cheeks, his shoulders stooped. Then slowly he straightened and faced me.

In a voice which was frightening in its calm control, he said:

"I have promised what I have promised. This cannot change that. You will be given safe passage out of Zorkada. You will leave my country and never return upon pain of horrible death!" The look in his eyes was harsh, hateful, but reined with such inner power that I could not but wonder

146

what kept him from killing me without so much as a word of explanation.

Then Illa came to me, trembling. Her arms slipped gently around my neck.

"Oh, Thoris, Thoris...I thought I had lost you..."

As I looked at her, I was sure I saw something in her eyes which was totally alien for the Princes of Haldolen. Could it be the suppressed emotion of love? I could hardly let myself believe this.

"Thank the Gods you are safe," I breathed. Then put my arms around her. She did not resist my embrace and in fact seemed to draw slightly closer. For a moment our lips were all but touching. I could feel her breath against my mouth, the fast rising and falling of her breasts, the beating of her heart.

All at once it seemed as if we were the only people on the room. I lost all awareness of everything other than the sweet nearness of Illa. It was a spell, but a natural one of the heart, given by the Gods in their generous love of lovers.

Without knowing what I was about to do, I kissed Illa. I crushed her madly against me with such violence and passion, such uncontrolled and painful demand within me that it would have been impossible for her to resist. Strangely, Illa did *not* resist, but instead returned the kiss with all the response of a woman in the arms of her lover.

A moment later, though, she pulled away, her face veiled over, and no expression showed to reveal her true thoughts.

I looked around the room to discover that the Wizard had left.

We were alone.

Illa suddenly asked in a very formal though shaky voice: "Why did you not accept Opil's offer? She would have made you a Lord and Wizard and given you honors which would have been beyond your wildest dreams." It was a strange statement but in character for her.

"But I thought you knew. Because I love you, Illa, my wonderful Princess." I moved to close the distance between us, afire with the belief that perhaps she returned my love. But she stopped me with a gentle hand on my chest.

"No, Thoris, it cannot be. You should have taken the offer of Opil, for in Haldolen, you are but a warrior and I a Princess!" She drew up her head, regal. Once more she was the royal Princess of my people; untouchable. "What you might wish, or think I might wish or desire, or even what I might wish, will never come to pass. It cannot be! Let us not forget this again." There was a pleading in her voice which was startling, as if she were struggling with herself, saying these words in order to convince herself as well.

"You must never do that again, never...for it cannot be!" she repeated.

For just a moment I believed that her control was about to break, for she leaned ever so slightly closer. Then she straightened and again became the royal daughter of Muda, Princess of Haldolen.

My mind was numb. I had never guessed it could be possible to win the love of Illa. I had never believed I would hold her dear form in my arms to kiss. Death would not be too high a price to pay for such a pleasure and honor; and such would have been my punishment if we were in Haldolen and her people discovered what had happened—for to touch the royal Princess in such a manner would have no other result. But that Illa might return my love was more than I would have dreamed possible. I could not help believe that she did. Maybe, in time, I told myself, anything might happen. Maybe someday she would offer her hand, her royalty and honors as did Opil. Maybe her father would reward me, and raise my station in life, so that Illa could openly reveal her true feelings to all the world. Such were my hopeful thoughts at that moment.

I finally nodded. "It is enough that I love you and that you know it. That will have to be enough for now."

She did not answer.

At that moment the voice of Xalla resounded loudly in the room.

"Your travel arrangements are complete. You will leave the Castle of Xalla forever. Now leave before the temper of my grief overcomes my honor and sends upon you the total destruction which my father's heart screams to make reality."

I took Illa's hand and she made no attempt to resist.

The Wizard stood in the entrance to the throne room, arm extended to indicate our passage.

He led the way down the hall in which the paintings of the Zorkadian warriors battled with their enemies and the Wizard worked death on all those who would challenge the safety of his land. Then beyond that to the outer entrance over which still hung the beautiful carved dragon-snake. I shuddered as we passed under it.

In the courtyard the Wizard stopped. My eyes opened wide with astonishment for there in front of us hung such a strange huge object as I had never seen or dreamed before. A leathery purple ball which filled the courtyard floated high in the air, held down by four huge ropes. A large metal basket hung under the ball.

Xalla spoke in staccato sentences. "This is a Floating Balloon. It will fly you over the lands of Zorkada. You can pass beyond the mountains. Stay in the basket. Direct the balloon by adjusting the four ropes. To land—you can do this only once—pull the rope in the middle. It lets out the air. It is simple. Now enter and be gone. *Fast!* " He hissed out that last with such violent hatred that I felt again a shiver of fear; for Xalla was a Wizard of great power. "I owed you more than one life. You took one from me. I return the debt. That is that!"

He moved us to the huge purple balloon which was some twenty heads wide and 50 heads high. The basket was about six heads in diameter and stocked with food and water.

"In. Now!" Xalla fairly cursed the words.

I helped the Princess into the basket and followed. Xalla once again instructed me on the handling of the balloon, which was amazingly simple. Anyone of the four ropes which hung down into the basket from above could be pulled and the balloon would move in that direction.

Then Xalla did a strange thing; just before he backed away. He said: "Thoris, you are a mighty warrior, and someday you will have all that you desire. I, Xalla, have spoken! I, Xalla, am saddened by the tragedy which has broken our friendship, and hold you not personally responsible. Good luck, and goodbye!" It was a grand gesture.

With that, Xalla took a sword from one of his servants and stepped to one of the lines which held the balloon grounded. He hacked at it as three other men did the same to the other lines.

I felt a lurch, and all at once the balloon rose like magic into the air. Its movement was amazingly fast and even before I realized it we were high above the Castle of Xalla, which was already rapidly receding.

The cold morning air shivered around our bodies but the sun was already coming up from the Eastern horizon, bringing light into a new day.

Illa stepped close to me as if in an effort to keep warm. For a moment our eyes met and there was no doubt about the emotion which welled up in Illa. No man has ever seen more love in the eyes of a woman he loves than I saw in that brief moment when the Princess of Haldolen was off her guard, displaying the truth of her feelings unmasked before me.

Then the moment was gone and she looked away. "We will soon be among our people, won't we?" There was a nostalgic choke in her voice.

I nodded. "Just over those high mountains to the East. By nightfall you will be safe in the colonies of Andus, and welcomed to the Palace of Dahsa, who will soon return you to your father."

She faced me then.

"Thoris," she murmured just above a soft whisper, "this, then, will be the last day we will ever be together thus. After today you will once again be a common warrior of my father's armies, and I the Princess of Haldolen and its colonies." She hesitated, as if the words were hard to speak. "But I want you to know that...that you have taught your Princess that there is little difference between the so-called common men of Haldolen and the royal men of her high station. Great men come from all levels of life—I know this to be true, now, because of you. And you are the greatest warrior of Haldolen that I have ever known. You are the kindest and bravest man I have ever heard of or known. And...the best man any woman could ever wish for."

150

Sudden tears were streaming down her cheeks. "If only...I were not a Princess..."

Then she suddenly came into my arms, her lips under mine, her body trembling. And I kissed her once more, for the last time, high over the lands of Zorkada, the forest slipping silently by, Fahda the Sun smiling upon us from the Eastern sky, as if blessing this moment which could not in the normal course of things ever repeat itself.

For a moment I was tempted to suggest that we never return to Haldolen but instead I rejected this, for even if Princess Illa were tempted and agreed, such a life would hold no true happiness. We would be running, and one cannot run from one's obligations, from one's self and conscience.

Finally, Illa reluctantly pulled away. She took my hand in hers.

"Today I will be but a woman called Illa, and you will be Thoris, Warrior of Haldolen, and we will pretend for a while that it can be like this forever."

And thus we moved aerially across the mountains, above their fog-covered peaks, and at last beyond, where the lands of Andus spread out in low, fruitful plains, where the high-peaked temples rose in holy honor of Muda, and Fahda the Sun, flying high in the skies in golden glory.

EPILOGUE

2006

If it weren't for Borgo Press, the following material would never have been added to this book, for it came into my hands too late for publication.

Shortly over a year after the *Swordmen of Vistar* was published, I received a small packet in the mail from Professor Bradford's daughter. It contained a note from her father and several other items dealing with what she called The Thoris Papers.

In part, her note to me said:

My father died a few months ago, just shortly after returning home from his trip to the Pacific Island dig. In his desk we discovered a file marked: HALDOLEN PROJECT, which contained the material here enclosed. It is very little, but I'm certain all of this will be of some interest to you.

Yours,

K. J. Bradford.

Enclosed with some handwritten notes, and Photostats, was a small, scribbled memo with my name on:

Charles—I have discovered far more than I had hoped. I now have in my possession what I call the Thoris Manuscript Scroll!

*A magnificent find. Far more than what I'd
seen before. At the dig I made an examination
of this ancient document—just here and there,
enough to get a marvelous hint at what it
might disclose. Stunning things are revealed!
About Haldolen; the world in which it existed;
the historical period of Thoris' life; and most
of all his continued adventures with Illa.
Sadly, much is missing. It is at least 32,000
years old! Amazing that even this much has
survived. Yet many portions are in mint condition!!! It has been impossible not to enjoy
these quick peeks back in Time; to see the
world through his eyes. But a serious translation will take years. So, like a child reading a
mystery novel, I couldn't help doing a translation of the closing section. Plus I knew
you'd want to see it. That's the least I can
share with you at this point.*

*Of course, when I've finished with the
total translation, I'll send you a copy.*

Your friend,

J. D. Bradford

I attempted to make contact with Ms. Bradford, but
she was, at the time, out of the country. A couple of years
later we did exchange a phone conversation in which she
said all the Thoris Files were in a university archives. All
attempts to translate the Thoris Scroll had failed. The key to
the translation had been locked in her father's brain. I
showed the Photostats I had to Dr. Donaldson (who, back in
1968 gave me the Noomas manuscript—to be released by
Wildside Press as *Torlo Hannis of Noomas*) but that drew a
blank, too. So matters remained until this year when Borgo
Press asked to see all the Photostats I have, and amazingly
was able to decipher most of them with a new computer pro-
gram one of their techies had created. But this revealed noth-

ing more than what the Professor's unedited translation notes offered.

So, here, then, are the final lines of Thoris' adventures with the Princess Illa.

—Charles Nuetzel
July 24, 2006

* * * * * * *

BRADFORD'S FINAL REPORT

The last part of the scroll in terrible condition, this much can be understood:

Apparently their balloon flight was brought to an end when a storm blew them off course and cast them into a strange, unnamed land.

> *[...] and smashed us (into) the cliffs.* Then after a black spot in the scroll: *[...] we entered the cave of the Mad(men) and [...]*

Just taunting hints of adventures now lost forever.

The very last lines are almost completely undamaged.

There are no details on how they actually reached Haldolen. At one point they were in a raft, drifting (down a river or across the ocean is not clear) then after some unreadable sections we find them in the Palace of Muda XI. Thoris was immediately arrested and held for over a day, then summoned before the mighty ruler of Haldolen. Since there is no description, we can only imagine the room, filled with people, the mighty Emperor of Haldolen sitting on his throne, Princess Illa, at his side.

Thoris had, early in their adventures, said to Illa in response to her royal fury at being commanded by a commoner: "Once you are safely in the hands of friends, you may punish me as you think proper for any offense for which I might be responsible."

Referring to that statement, the Princess now said, stepping forward to stare unemotionally at Thoris:

"Imagine [...] how humiliating it was being ordered around like a slave-girl by such a low ranking warrior! It is quite unforgivable! [...]"

Why was Illa acting so strangely, so distant and coldly regal? Had she changed so much in just one day at the hands of her father and his court? This reversal made a mockery of the last couple of years. I had been, apparently, nothing but a necessary unpleasant pawn to [...]. She had always been unpredictable; perhaps her admissions of love had just been cruel lies, desperate attempts to keep what she truly thought of as a disgustingly commonplace companion [...]. Now, once again home, in her father's Royal court and protection, there was no longer any need to pretend.

This seemed the only explanation. My disappointment mixed with a welling sense of confusion. The long hours of confinement, without food or water, awaiting this audience with the ruler of Haldolen, had drained what little reserve the last weeks of our journey had left me. If I was to be punished for my services and my honesty, the sooner they [...] Obvious it had been a mistake to have admitted my love for her, but I had foolishly believed I was speaking to the woman, not some Ice Princess without human feelings.

The mighty God-Lord of all Haldolen, Muda XI, glared at me, demanded: "What do

say to these (charges)? Have you dared to
[...]"

    [...] was my reply.

    [...] he (said, turning) to his daughter.

    [...] Illa (now) stood in front of me, so
close I could (have easily) pulled her into my
arms as [...]. But this was the Royal Lady of
Haldolen; untouchable—and hardly the
"slave girl" who had so passionately declared her love for me.

    "He treated me as a common slave!"
Her voice projected loudly, so that all those in
the Royal Court could hear these damning
words. "Can you imagine that? And actually
come into physical contact with me so many
times..."

    "In saving your life!" I blurted, not
even caring what they thought. I was unable
to believe these harsh, unfair words were being uttered by the lips of the woman I had so
worshipped since that very first day on the
galley ship Vayis.

    "Silence!" Muda XI stated, as if
squashing an annoying bug.

    Illa brushed my words away with a
Royal wave of her hand. Then she continued
in that loud, regal voice, condemning me before the presence of the mass of people gathered to witness these proceedings. "A crime,
mind you, that would bring instant death if he
were to do so right now!"

    A murmuring sound of approval ap-
plauded this statement and her father nodded,
face grim as it studied mine.

    "Quite right," Muda XI announced,
loudly. "But, of course we can not totally ignore the service that he did perform in returning you to [...]."

    "Yes, but for crimes against me he
must pay the full price!" Illa stated.

"Crimes?" I blurted out like a savage beast who has been mortally wounded by its mate. "Crimes! What crimes? You'd be dead—"

Illa ignored me, but her father exclaimed: "Silence, warrior!" Then to Illa, he inquired: "What, then, is your judgment concerning these crimes against our Royal House, and against you as Princess of all Haldolen? You must command the punishment."

Without hesitation she said: "There are only two possibilities: Death in the most horrible manner or something even more...appalling and longer lasting!"

"What would be more appalling than death?" Her father sounded honestly surprised.

"The matter we talked about this morning!" she announced with loud finality.

[...]

—and Illa was standing very close to me, looking up into my eyes as if trying to read my thoughts. In a voice only I could hear, she stated, rather flatly: "Now you learn, warrior, the true feeling of the woman you claimed to so worship and love! You are about to discover the extent of my Royal pleasure as to your just punishment!"

A slight smile turned on her lips as she half whispered that to me. Then, very loudly, so all would hear, she proclaimed: "I demand that Thoris of Rota be given Royal Status! Only then can he avoid swift death as [...]"

"It is done!" Muda XI said turning to the Court Recorder sitting a short distance from him [...] "Predate this Royal Status as of his date of birth!"

Then to his daughter, face very grim: "Now, that done...we must remember, beyond insults you suffered, there is a matter of your honor! For more than two years this man was your sole companion!"

"Yes..." she murmured, her shoulder almost touching mine. "My honor."

There was a long, drawn out silence, and my eyes took in the expressions of those men and woman around me. For the first time I began to notice the mockery in the eyes as they met mine.

"I accept, father, your judgment and considered wisdom in this matter!" She seemed to be standing far too close to me. It would have been easy to break her lovely neck!

Muda XI glanced at me, said: "And you, Thoris of Rota, will now submit totally to my just proclamation!"

"Or die most horribly!" Illa promised softly, [...] for the first time so very close that I could feel the warmth of her body [...].

Muda XI's expression hardly (changed?) as he announced: "So it will be immediately written in the Royal Records of Haldolen...For services rendered and...all those previous womanly complaints...this man standing before us shall now accept his richly deserved...life sentence...To save our Royal Honor, Thoris of the Haldolen Court shall be joined with this conniving young lady, Princess Illa, in marriage for eternity! So it is now recorded!"

The roar of approval was hardly heard. My attention had been completely captivated by Illa as her face lifted, lips parted, eyes shamelessly challenging me to kiss her right there in front of all the court to see. "Dare you, my Royal Thoris of Rota, claim your just punishment for services rendered?"

SWORDMEN OF VISTAR, BY CHARLES NUETZEL

I (enclosed) her in (my) arms [...] and our lips touched [...] as she clung to me [...] trembling in...[...}

ABOUT THE AUTHOR

Charles Nuetzel was born in San Francisco in 1934, and writes:

"As long as I can remember I wanted to be a writer. It was a dream I never thought would materialize. But with the help of Forrest J Ackerman, who became my agent, I managed to finally make it into print.

"I was lucky enough not only in selling my work to publishers but also ending up packaging books for some of them, and finally becoming a 'publisher' much like those who had bought my first novels. From there it as a simple leap to editing not only a science-fiction anthology, but also a line of SF books for Powell Sci-Fi back in the 1960s. Throughout these active professional years I had the chance to design some covers and do graphic cover layouts for pocket books & magazines."

Much of his work in covers and graphics are a result of having had a father who was a professional commercial artist, and who did a number of covers for sci-fi magazines in the 1950s and later for pocket books—even for some of Mr. Nuetzel's books.

In retirement he has become involved in swing dancing, a long time lover of Big Band jazz. But more interestingly world travels have taken him (and his wife Brigitte) across the world, to Hawaii, Caribbean, Mexico, Kenya, Egypt, Peru, having a lifelong interest in ancient civilizations. His website is full of thousands of pictures taken during these trips.